# Gravy

# Gravy

Ron Singer

*Dedicated to the old, and to the old at heart.*

# CONTENTS

"After seventy, it's all gravy."
—Elsie Yamin, the Author's Mother-in-Law (1901-1978)

# INTRODUCTION

THIS, FROM A memoir I wrote about my mother's family:

"There are few things I hate more than stories about lonely, impoverished oldsters sitting by their windows feeling bored and bereft. I don't even like these characters when they turn up in English murder novels as the neighborly snoops who peep through the curtains for twenty years until, one fatal day, they see something which solves the whole case. They, and the writers, for that matter, should get a life. Anyway, they, the writers need better plots."

"Get a life." "Better plots." Easy for me to say. But what I think I was really doing here was a kind of unconscious boasting, the subtext being, "*I have* a life." Indeed, like Chaucer's Wife from beside Bath, "I have had my world, as in my time." Of course, older people can be as sarcastic as anyone else about what constitutes "a life." Take the following hospital anecdote, in which the narrator and the rabbi might both deny the other's claim to real existence.

## 2012:

IN A NEW York hospital, with almost-kidney failure, I shared a room with an Orthodox rabbi suffering from chronic, multiple complaints. As (Tuesday) evening fell, his wife reluctantly left for the five-hour bus ride back up to Monsey: she did not drive. "Don't forget my pants," he reminded her. (Presumably, they left as few things as possible in the hospital room.) The next day, ten bus hours and a short night's rest later, she was back. Cutting through all the red tape for his discharge took hours. Finally cleared, and anxious to leave, he snatched the pants from the shopping bag in which she had brought them. They were beautiful, dark blue, possibly made of silk. "Oh, no!" he cried in horror. "You brought my *Shabbos* pants!" I can't remember the resolution. Did he wear the Shabbos pants, desecrating them? Or did she hurry out to buy him another pair?

Moral: "Strait is the gate, and narrow is the way."

**GRAVY** IS DIVIDED into five thematic, overlapping sections: Accountancy, Books, Activism, Families (Surrogate), and Families (Real). I could have added a sixth, Death and Dying, but, as the first quotation (*supra*) suggests, I mean to minimize morbidity. Even so, death, dying, and many other tropes of aging, such as humor, cultural change, egotism, and marginalization, will show up in these portraits of Gravy-dom.

Readers should also note that all utterances or descriptions that are sexist, racist, or otherwise offensive do not reflect the author's values or opinions. They should be blamed on the character who expresses them, in many cases a benighted curmudgeon whose values and opinions have been rendered anachronistic by social and political change. As one of the characters remarks, hindsight is a form of ignorance.

# I. ACCOUNTANCY

"The economy, Stupid!"
–James Carville, 1992[1]


"No man but a blockhead ever wrote except for money."
–Dr. Johnson[2].


THAT MY GOOD friend Bob Shepard was a Certified Public Accountant (CPA) may have contributed to his belated longing to get a life. The fiasco that resulted from this longing took place in April 2016, shortly after Bob had reached the Age of Gravy. As the reader will see, I was personally implicated in the fiasco.


## Secrets of the Boardwalk

IT ALL STARTED when Bob's wife, Amy, told my wife, Liz, her confidante, that she was worried about her husband. On two consecutive days he had, uncharacteristically, wandered off alone. The first morning, out of the blue, he had announced his intention of taking the day off and riding the subway out to Coney Island, "for a walk on the boardwalk." Since the couple normally went to C.I. in tandem, and since Amy had to work that day (office manager for a law firm), she urged Bob to wait for the weekend. But he refused.

---

[1] This oft-quoted aphorism is found, for instance, in
https://en.wikipedia.org/wiki/It%27s_the_economy,_stupid

[2] www.brainyquote.com/quotes/samuel_johnson_170103

The next day, he went again. That evening, as they were having dinner, his nose red from the spring sunshine and the depleted ozone layer, he made a speech that Amy interpreted as a semi-confession. Or, as she put it, "His sunburnt nose kept getting longer."

Liz, who has a near-phonographic memory, quoted Amy's account of Bob's semi-confession: "'Boy, you wouldn't believe the characters you run into on the boardwalk these days—junkies, winos, Three Card Monte sharps, restaurant touts who practically mug you. I even saw *a couple of teen-aged prostitutes pretending to be fortune-tellers.* [Italics mine.] They had a card table, costumes, the works. Can you beat that?'"

For Amy, the last part had been the kicker: "'The way he described those girls, the look on his face…fur*tive*…I smelled a *ve*ry big rat.'"

Bob was a 71-year old CPA who kept postponing his retirement. He owned a small business specializing in the personal income taxes of people in the arts. (He did ours.) Anything but "furtive," Bob normally sounded like an accountant: precise, laconic, on the dry side. Since he had been extremely busy for the two or three months leading up to the end of tax season, it was easy to see why he had wanted to stretch his legs and suck in some sea air and sunshine. But, obviously, Amy didn't see it that way.

"I think she's right," was Liz's verdict.

"No opinion."

The next day, putting their heads together, the women hatched a plot to find out whether there was fire behind the smoke—a plot that involved *me*. As Liz explained at breakfast that morning, "See if you can draw him into a man-to-man confessional, Ron. Think of it as a chance to make positive use of those world-class social skills you're always bragging about. You know, have a few drinks…tell him about the time…"

Uh, oh, I thought: here it comes. She was going to bring up the passionate kiss I had admitted to having shared with a sexy young acolyte at a book party five years ago. Well, she did bring it up, but thankfully, without the pain and rancor that had greeted the original confession. I'll say this for Liz: she wields a mean wit, but she's not like that Marx sister, Carpo. (Or is it Carpa?) Even better, I was relieved that the old kiss was *all* she brought up.

"Sure," I said. "Why not?"

Soon, she bustled off to her studio. (Liz is a painter, retired from her day job as an art teacher.) As I got ready to call Bob, a few stubborn facts kept me from following her plan of attack. Although the four of us occasionally went out for brunch together, and although Bob and I sometimes took walks, we never met for drinks. So, to keep him from smelling a rat of his own, I would do this *my* way.

"Beautiful day, eh, Bob?"

"Good morning, Ron. Yes, indeed. Spring has finally sprung."

"You must be glad tax season is over."

"And how."

"How about a walk in the Botanical Gardens today? I hear the cherry blossoms are out. You available?"

"Sounds good," he said. "Actually, I promised Joe I'd look over an audit notice he got from the IRS. But there's no hurry, I'm not even going to charge him."

"That's very generous of you. Hey, I have an even better idea. Let's take the train out to Brighton. We can have lunch at that Bukharin place with the big Plaster-of-Paris pierogi outside, then walk to Coney Island on the boardwalk."

"Actually, I was just there last week, Ron. Twice, in fact."

Time to cut to the chase. "Ah ha! So you don't want to go again? I can certainly understand why, after what happened to you with those two prost—"

"'After what *happened* to me? Nothing *happened*, Ron. Amy told Liz about that?"

"Yep. She said something about a pair of what I believe are called "hoes" tricked out as fortune-tellers."

"Well, yes." There was a brief pause. "But so what? Sure, let's go for a walk on the boardwalk."

"Great."

By now, I wanted to end this conversation, which was making *me* feel like the guilty party. Maybe Liz was right and uncovering the truth about Bob's boardwalk adventures would require more finesse than I had realized.

* * *

SINCE WE LIVE only a few blocks apart, Bob and I agreed to meet at a nearby subway entrance in half an hour. Twenty-nine minutes later, I arrived at the station to find him already waiting. Hurrying down the stairs, we caught a Brighton Beach-bound B-train. Since the MTA was doing their usual massive infrastructure repairs, we sped past some half-renovated stations without stopping, which made the long trip somewhat shorter. Isn't it always like that when you're not in a hurry?

This particular subway line goes back and forth between underground and elevated. When it is elevated, it runs above neighborhoods of great variety, ranging from tree-lined streets with big, fancy, stand-alone homes, to commercial districts featuring discount this-and-that stores, to industrial parks full of rooftop graffiti and deserted-looking factories. In some places, every sign is in Chinese. Brooklyn is an exhilarating place to travel through—fast. Since neither of us had brought along a book, we shared Bob's paper, which we then left on the train, so (as he put it) "some lucky stranger can save $2.50."

A few minutes before noon, we reached Brighton Avenue, and climbed down the long flight of stairs to 6th Street. I love going to B.B. I have never visited Odessa, but I imagine it could be the model for this bustling, vaguely nefarious commercial artery. It's always a pleasure to be back in Old New York, for here you can still find real commercial enterprises—good, cheap restaurants, greengrocers, naughty nightclubs, cavernous ethnic food stores, and exotic clothing emporia. If it's not too late, may God protect B.B. from gentrification.

Bob and I walked the four short blocks south to 2nd Street, and turned right, toward the big pierogi. But when we got there, to our disappointment, we were assaulted through the window by what sounded like the soundtrack from a Central Asian softcore porn video. We could also see that all five tables were occupied.

"Let's take our walk first," I suggested. "We can grab a hot dog at Nathan's."

"Sounds good. Get a little exercise before our unhealthy lunch."

Even on the side street, we could feel a stiff, chilly wind blowing in from the ocean. Although we were both sensibly dressed, I worried that we would freeze our butts off. At the boardwalk, we turned right again, toward C.I. Pushing against the crosswinds, we must have made a funny couple. Bob is about six-two, and stoops, trudging along with his hands clasped behind his back. Two or three inches shorter, I'm "bulky" (i.e. biggish gut), and I take quick little steps, like a kid learning to roller skate. Liz says I look as if I'm running away from something. (My shadow? My past?)

I had last visited B.B. (with her) about two years back, right before the city suffered the devastation of Hurricane Sandy. As

Bob and I hurried along now, some of the changes I noticed may have been Sandy-related. The ocean side of the boardwalk was dotted with new, one-story, very solid-looking buildings on stout concrete poles. Although there were no signs or other indications of their purpose, I guessed that they were hurricane-proof restrooms, the proverbial brick shit houses, except that there were other buildings marked as restrooms, on the landward side.

Down on the beach, in addition to a few walkers and joggers, there was a large gathering of seagulls, forming an amoeba in the sand. They looked as if they had been shot out of the sky

"Birds of a feather," I quipped, "drop together. What are they doing there?"

"Enjoying the sunshine," Bob opined. "Like us."

Since it was a weekday, and not yet the busy season, traffic on the boardwalk was thin. Thin, in two senses, in number and, I could have sworn, girth: there seemed to be fewer jumbo Russians than in summer. Nor was there as good a selection of the hilariously garish outfits I always enjoy at B.B. But there were still a few doozies, such as a middle-aged peroxide blonde wearing a blue, fake-fur vest over a paisley kaftan.

The demographic that day seemed deceptively like the peaceable kingdom. On a basketball court in a playground on the landward side (BB at B.B.), I saw a pale, fat boy who, although hatless, looked Jewish. He was gesticulating, and I heard him shout, "Paco. Paco! Pass it to Mohammed! Shoot, Mohammed! Shoot!"

Mohammed, a gawky boy wearing large, black-rimmed glasses, launched a clunker off the side of the backboard. These boys apparently belonged to the Bricklayers Union. At seventy-two, I could still have schooled them in the art of the jump shot.

Halfway to Coney Island, spotting an empty bench facing the ocean, we decided to ignore the wind and rest for a bit. By this point, I must say, I was disappointed that we had not encountered the fortune-tellers. I pictured two young cuties seated at a card table wearing turbans and leather hot pants. As if we were oxygen-deprived, Bob and I sucked in the sea air.

Then, suddenly, there they were, bookending us on our bench, squeezing us together: Showtime. They must have been eighteen or nineteen. One was a faux-redhead, the other a faux-blonde. They were heavily made up, siliconized, and wearing enough perfume to Ralph Laurenify "the multitudinous seas"— i.e., I could no longer smell the salty air. They were dressed not as fortune-tellers, but like models posing as professional athletes: spandex running-suits in shocking pastels, and Day-Glo multi-colored running shoes. Instead of turbans, they both sported bright orange baseball caps, worn backwards.

"Hello there, Mr. Bob, baby," said the blonde, who had plopped down on his end. Her accent combined Russian with Brooklynese, making the greeting sound like, "Alloo there, Meezterr Pob, pay-bee." You get the idea.

"And, also, hello to you, also, Meezter Zexie," said the redhead, a contralto, flashing a high-wattage smile and poking me with an elbow.

"Aren't you going to introduce us to your friend?" asked the blonde. Not waiting for him to reply, she added, "How about going under the boardwalk again, Bobby? I think you loved that big kiss I gave you the other day—didn't you, you naughty boy? Or this time, maybe something a beet more…serious?"

"Perhaps, you would also like, also, to go under the boardwalk, with me, Mr. Pob's Nice Friend," suggested the redhead. "A wonderful soul kiss for only ten dollars, if you're too scary to do anything else." She winked at me.

"Or too chip," added the blonde. They laughed uproariously.

"'Oh, when the sub goess dowwwn…'" they sang, in unison, dissolving into more laughter.

Bob blushed vermilion. "Not today, girls. I'm still dizzy from last time," he added, in a weak attempt at levity. Wearing what can only be called a shit-eating half grin, he turned and winked at me.

Well, that cat had finally sprung from the bag. Amy had been right, after all—sort of. Poor Bob. All he had done, apparently, was to buy a kiss, just like we boys used to do at those carnival booths in the innocent old days. Except, back then, it had cost a nickel.

To make the rest of this long story short, I extricated us from the girls by tossing them a few compliments, and ten bucks apiece, "for lunch money." We left them on the bench, shouting lewd suggestions and blowing kisses after us as we hurried off. By the time I looked back, both of them were texting away furiously. No signs of a card table or crystal ball.

The rest of the "outing" went pretty much as could be expected. We ate under an umbrella at Nathan's (the smaller one, on the boardwalk), trying to warm our hands with hot coffee, which we did not drink, for fear of being unable to sleep that night. (They didn't have decaf.) I enjoyed my hot dog, but Bob did not look as if he enjoyed his—at all.

* * *

THUS CONCLUDES THE day's adventures of Ron and Bob, two typical men of a certain age. All that remains to be said is that, on the way home, I easily persuaded Bob to confess his peccadillo to Amy. You may be able to guess how I managed this. After swearing him to secrecy, I told him about the hottie I was "seeing" in the Bronx. He swallowed his teeth. Then, realizing that my sin dwarfed his peccadillo, he unswallowed them. If Bob and I had not been friends for life before, we were now. (By the way, I really had been "seeing" a Bronx hottie, but the boardwalk adventure made me stop. I realized that, alas, I was getting too old for that kind of stuff.)

* * *

FOR FAIRNESS' SAKE, the end of this story will be told from the wives' point of view, which I can imagine.

The next day, Liz and Amy are in their respective workplaces, talking on their cell phones. As Amy recounts Bob's spluttered confession, employing elaborate, hilarious mimicry, the women almost die of laughter. When she finishes, there is a pause. Neither of them wants to get back to work. This is too much fun.

"You know, Liz," Amy remarks, "your Ron is so clever and persuasive…cute, too. Quite a guy. In fact, I'd be surprised if he never…"

Liz clears her throat. "Now, now, that's not nice, dear. Let's not go there." And, closing their phones, they leave it at that.

**The End**

PURSUANT TO THE subject of money (accountancy), here is a pithy poem that takes us back (way back) along the corridors of time.

## Pocketbook Money Keys

## (a double sonnet)

That, according to my doting mother
(and this in the days before her dotage),
was my first, connected utterance,
and, according to me, who loves Linguistics,
was an instance of telegraphic speech.
If, as she said, I said it at ten months,
it would, indeed, have shown the precocity
of her ten-month darling, for "normally"
telegraphy occurs between eighteen
and thirty-six months. Since studies suggest
that the telegraphic, or "two-word," stage,
typically combines a verb and a noun,
my noun string must have been an outlier.
Never mind! The phrase remains iconic,

or, at least, a phrase I don't forget,
as I embark upon my own dotage.
The reason I remember it, perhaps,
is that it's fixed in long-term memory.
But, soon, I'll need devices to keep me
from losing my pocketbook, money, keys,
which, themselves, morph into devices: apps.
Since the memory-theater method, where

symbolic places and objects evoked
huge swaths of learning, no longer works,
I depend (as does my wife) on lists,
and on strict placement of essentials—pills—
which I lay out on the kitchen table.
The trick is to tell intention from act.


Bob Shepard's misadventure and my forgetfulness are examples of the embarrassments that seem endemic to the Age of Gravy. Have you ever had a dream where you found yourself naked in an elevator? Something like that happened to Dave Schaaf, another friend of mine. Dave's experience illustrates a sub-theme of Accountancy: the scams young people devise to bilk *Golden* Agers.

This time, I served as the Watson to Dave's Holmes, the Boswell to his Dr. Johnson. As the course of events unfolded, Dave, who is a widower, poured his heart out to me, over several cups of coffee (decaf). Unlike my big part in "Secrets of the Boardwalk," here I am limited to a cameo, the character called Common Sense, or C.S. The circumstantial nature of this story, not to mention the drastic jump in POV near the end, may cause the reader (you) to smell a rat. The rat's name is Poetic License.


## Other People's Clothes

NO DOUBT ABOUT it, they were *his*. If it had been just one garment—say, the long-sleeved, collarless, light blue shirt—it might have been coincidence. But the white duck pants with the frayed cuffs and the big spot from the dropped raspberry on the left knee? The ancient, torn, khaki baseball cap with the black brim skewed to the left? No, they were *Dave's* clothes, his *stolen* clothes.

Not that they looked bad on the thief. She was a slender young blonde, about five-nine, the same height as he was. When she stretched her arms toward the beautiful blue sky…well, let's just say, if Dave had done that, he didn't think many heads would have turned. Ditto for the removal of her (his) clothes and the slathering of her body with oil, in preparation for a bout of sunbathing.

"Thief?" Dave would certainly never call anyone that without cause, not even if the person-in-question had been another balding seventy-something. But the reason he thought "thief" was that, the day before, his clothes had disappeared from an unlocked locker at the Health Club. Why had the locker been unlocked? He had left the lock at home in the drawer in which he kept several plastic bags full of miscellaneous items.

* * *

WHEN HE HAD finished his workout—half an hour on the stationary bike, then fifty "crunches" (twitches, really)—and returned to the locker room to shower, the clothes were gone, all of them. Luckily, he always kept his wallet and keys with him during the workout, so he hadn't lost those. The showering materials—shampoo, soap, sandals, and towel—were also right where he had left them, on the shelf above the now denuded clothes hooks. And the thief had spared his shoes, which sat side by side beneath the hooks.

Luckily, too, it was a warm afternoon. So he wrapped the soap, shoes, and shampoo in the unused towel, and, still wearing his sweaty gym clothes, scurried home to his apartment two blocks away. There, he showered, donned substitute attire and, recovering from the shock of being robbed, called the Club to report the theft.

The young man who picked up was very polite, tolerating without interruption the caller's weak threats and his diatribe about the debauched times in which they lived. When Dave had spent himself, the clerk promised to call back as soon as he could "solve the problem."

"Yeah, right," Dave thought. He remembered a now-deceased lawyer friend having mentioned that those "Not Responsible for…" signs, one of which was prominently displayed at the entrance to the locker room, did not actually shield institutions from liability. Their purpose, the friend explained, was to make people more cautious and, if push came to shove, to discourage lawsuits.

* * *

IT WAS A bright, hot Sunday afternoon in mid-August. When Dave arrived at the beach, the only parking spot he was able to find in the huge lot was in the second row from the back. After threading his way past hundreds of cars, he trudged across the sand, which was a mine field of elaborate picnics, multiple kamikaze sporting events like Frisbee and touch football in particularly crowded areas, and competing boom boxes, which made the place sound like an open-air electronics store. Halfway to the water, he finally found a space, which turned out to be twenty yards from the young woman. From the vantage point of his small mesh-and-aluminum folding chair, experiencing the shock of recognition, he saw the stolen garments.

"Stolen?" What other explanation could there be? "Sorry, my boyfriend happened to be wearing the same clothes as you, and he must have left his in the locker right next to yours. Did you look?"

"Piss on my head," Dave might have riposted, "but don't tell me it's raining." He had heard that one about four decades before, during basic training at Fort Bragg, North Carolina. Luckily, the Vietnam War had ended before he could be deployed.

25

The question was how the young woman had gotten hold of his clothes. Since there was no way she could have stolen them from the men's locker room at the Club, maybe it was the boyfriend, and he had loaned her the purloined garments as a beach [sic] cover up.

After ten minutes of uncertainty, Dave decided to accost her. She now lay face down on a blanket, propped on her elbows, and reading a magazine. Gathering his things, he inched forward, pretending to be looking for a new spot, and thinking that the throng provided good cover. Halfway to the young woman, he stopped, and a football whizzed past his ear, presumably because the "QB" had anticipated that he would keep moving.

"Sorry," he heard from a tall, hefty boy who was working on a major league sunburn.

"No problem," he replied. (Isn't that what people said nowadays?)

But he realized that he did, in fact, have a problem, which was the reason he had stopped: how should he approach the young woman?

Possible opening: "Oh, hello. Aren't those my clothes on your blanket?"

Likely reply #1: "Give me a break, Gramps. You some kind of fetishist?"

Likely reply #2: "Huh? I mean, guys are always trying to get into my pants, but I never heard that one before."

A different approach: "Excuse me, Miss—Ms.—do you mind if I ask where you bought those clothes?"

Likely reply: "Why? You want to go shopping in the same store? Get lost, fool."

It dawned on him that this was a situation where there was no right thing to say.

Common Sense: "Just forget about it, Dave. No point having a coronary over some worn-out old rags."

Reply: "Excuse me? Those aren't 'some worn-out old rags.' They're my favorite, most comfortable, everyday warm-weather clothes."

C.S.: "Boohoo. Then think of a smart way to get them back."

Reply: "Hmm."

When in doubt, go slow. Inching forward again, Dave spotted a space not more than twenty feet from the lovely thief. Why, you ask, was this space available? Because of its proximity to a garbage bin, which had been tipped over. Skirting the reeking mess, he carefully set up his chair, and waited. For what, he did not know. Afraid he might lose her, he did not even venture into the surf.

Half an hour later, the young woman glanced at her phone, stood up, and did the strip tease in reverse, donning the purloined garments. It was time to act—sort of. Gathering his own things, Dave followed her, as unobtrusively as possible, to the parking lot. When she reached the third row, suggesting an early arrival, she unlocked her car, an aging domestic banger, and put her things in the trunk.

Memorizing the plate number, Dave walked back to his own car (a newer, Japanese model), where he copied the number onto the back of a credit card receipt. Dumping his things on the back seat and resisting an impulse to try to follow the other car, he exited the lot and joined the moderate-to-heavy Sunday afternoon traffic.

✳ ✳ ✳

WHEN HE GOT home, after some leftover rotisserie chicken, Dave enjoyed an old black-and-white film noir on PBS, then fell asleep trying to forget the clothes. The next morning, he did the usual: breakfast, dishes, make the bed, fuss with email. At this point, the phone rang. It was the clerk from the Health Club, calling, no doubt, to express his regrets. But after a few courtesies, he cut to the surprising chase:

"Good news about your clothes, sir. I'm happy to report that we've located them. This is what appears to have happened. When a client leaves possessions of any kind in an unlocked locker, the attendant is instructed to remove them. We then secure the items in the lost-and-found closet, which is located to the rear of the locker room, on the left as you come in. We follow this procedure because, like everyone else these days, har har, we do suffer the occasional theft."

Although he was totally baffled, Dave said nothing. Had the young woman's clothes really been a coincidence? Was it even possible that the raspberry stain on her pants had been *her* raspberry stain, or something else? But he was afraid that mentioning the beach episode might make the young man think he was crazy.

The fellow nattered on. "Since our attendants perform frequent sweeps of the locker room, what must have happened, sir, is that your clothes were removed for safeguarding while you were busy enjoying your workout."

Dave finally piped up. "But shouldn't they have left a note, or something? So people will know?"

"Excellent suggestion, sir. Next time you come in, why don't you write that down on one of the slips we provide at the front desk, and drop it in the suggestion box? And, of course, you can also pick up your clothes. For security purposes, we will, however, ask that you bring along a picture I.D., such as a valid driver's license, and that you describe the lost items. I'm sure you understand the reason for these precau—oops. Sorry. I have a call on the other line. Please hold."

"Bye," Dave replied hastily. "See you later."

"…nice day, sir," said the clerk, also hastily.

After lunch and a short, restless nap, still puzzled, Dave gathered his gear (lock included), walked over to the Club, and hurried to the lost-and-found. Describing the clothes, and displaying his driver's license to the older African-American man on duty, he was silently handed a large, neatly folded clear plastic bag. Everything seemed to be there, and the garments had even been laundered—unfortunately, with perfumed detergent. When he checked more carefully, however, the left knee of his pants no longer had the raspberry stain. Stranger and stranger…

With a shrug, he changed, then put both sets of clothes into a locker, and carefully secured it. Trying hard to keep his mind free and clear, he joined the post-weekend repentance crowd in the room with the machines, where he proceeded to a particularly vigorous workout. When he returned to the locker room, his foolish fantasy that the clothes had disappeared again proved to be just that. He showered, dressed, and, carrying the plastic bag, to which he added his workout kit, left the Club, nodding to the young man at the front desk, who was absorbed in an intense phone conversation.

* * *

"HEY, BABE, IT'S me. Has that old fart picked up his clothes yet? Everything cool?"

"No thanks to you, Ginny," replied the clerk. "I mean, I left you the message Saturday night, and it took you twenty-four hours to bring the stuff back? And the damn things reeked of suntan oil. We had to run them through the washing machine three times."

"OMG. I already told you, George, I went out Saturday night, and I was at the beach all day yesterday, and I forgot my phone at home. I mean, I brought the damn clothes back as soon as I saw your text."

George lowered his voice and muffled the receiver with his hand. "Give me a break, Ginny. You expect me to believe you didn't check your phone messages for twenty-four hours?" He drew a ragged breath. "Okay, let's forget that small untruth. But there's a lesson here: no more boosting from unlocked lockers. That's it. I mean, it was nice while it lasted—the fancy watches, designer threads—but I mean, this may be a crap job, but it's the only job I have."

"Okay, okay, George. Peace. I'm a reformed woman. And to celebrate, suppose I take you out for Chinese tonight. Meet me at the office at, say, seven?"

"Roger, will do, sir—I mean, ma'am."

* * *

SO THAT WAS that. Dave got his favorite warm-weather clothes back, and the young woman at the beach gradually faded into a not unpleasant memory—or yet another chapter in the Annals of Bewilderment. As for the two thieves, having learned that job loss and possible incarceration for stealing vintage garments and accessories was childish, they were now hastening along the road to maturity. So for the moment, at least, everyone was happy. No harm, no foul. Am I right?

## The End

TURNING AWAY FROM the foibles of my friends, here is a long lampoon, also about money. Although this one, too, features an accountant, it is cut from whole cloth. Oh, but first, another brief, thematically relevant interlude, an aria from my libretto for *Rimshot*, an opera about the money-driven world of rock music. The singer, whom I imagine as being on the cusp of the Age of Gravy, is the manager of a rock group and, stereotypically, of Scottish descent.

## The Money Aria

Stewart:
In childhood it's common
For dreams to recur
Til fixed in memory.
Mine was of money,
Money…quarters,
Money…dimes,
Money…nickels,
Money…
Childish treasure
Found on the sidewalk
As I would walk along.

In what sense dreams are omens,
I leave to the wise.
Only know that as Manager
Of the world-renowned Tumescents,
In some sense I feel
My wealth comes from the gutter.
But not to bite the hand that feeds me,

I know the band needs me.
For these babes-in-the-woods
I'm the one who gets the goods:
Royalties, residuals,
Rights audio-visual…
To play hundreds of cities,
Theaters, parks, ball fields…
Takes logistical genius
And consummate greed.
Yes, when it comes to fast talk,
Stewart is your man.
But this is not a cake-walk,
For a rock band on tour's like a family on vacation,
The children's complaints are depressingly frequent.
Here is no honest, uplifting vocation.
Diaper-changer to five scruffy delinquents.
Diaper-changer…Stewart is your man, Stewart is your man.


## The Actuarialist

Note: Actuarial jargon and all data that are real, rather than invented, come from National Vital Statistics Reports for 2000 and from the web sites of several actuarial schools and professional organizations.


*PROSPECTUS*

Brandon Flicker (GradCertActSt, MActSt), President and
CEO, Actuarialist Life Solutions, Inc.tm
brflk@actlife.com

# I. Introductory

*Note : Since prospective clients who read this brochure are unlikely to recognize the term "actuarialist," ᵗᵐ I offer the following definitional and biographical notes to enhance transparency and to establish my bona fides.*

## IA. Definitional

What, then, is an actuarialist ᵗᵐ? In layman's terms, using the same stochastic and other statistical models as an actual actuary, an actuarialist offers consultations to private parties which provide accurate data relevant to specific plans and dreams, including, where relevant, data for life expectancy.  The actuarialist thereby facilitates realistic estimates of clients' chances of bringing said plans and dreams to fruition, with or without considerations of mortality.

## IB. Biographical

In 2002, after a nine-year stint in the insurance "game," which followed immediately upon graduation from college, nine years which constituted my entire, unique opportunity to experience, for better or worse, the state of being a twenty-something … *I had had it!* Nine years of brain-frying study through a series of eleven grueling examinations which together brought me to maximum rank and salary in what has been rated the first or second-most desirable profession (ha!) in this, our great nation. Nine years of significantly bloating the bottom line of a major conglomerate (the name-brand recognition of which I will not now enhance by either identification or excoriation) which specializes in annuities and in property and casualty insurance. Nine years of stochastically calibrating rates for policies ranging from property and liability for a large, modern, wooden vacation structure with concrete-block foundation and no cellar, eight-hundred yards from the ocean in an environment of moderate-to-high hurricane activity; to a term annuity with survivors' rights for a fifty-something who is currently fit and practicing a healthy lifestyle, but who smoked cigarettes (an average of 1.7 packs per day, filtered) from age sixteen until he suffered a minor infarction at forty-one, and whose family tree features on both primary branches rates of smoking-related lung cancer and coronary disease which are of statistically significant elevation. In short, to repeat, *I had had it!*

In as much as my present purpose is only incidentally biographical, having just sketched in  the years of my life from ages 22 to 30 (by which point my remaining life expectancy was 46.4), I will stint even further upon the intermediate steps: the personal crisis which precipitated my resignation; the terms of said resignation (i.e., the gold-plated parachute); my motives for entering, or rather for inventing, my current profession (independence and altruism); and all financial and logistical details of my current operation other than the fee structure delineated in Section 3 (see below) of this prospectus.


## 2. Examples

**Note:** In order to provide prospective clients with some sense of the parameters of what an actuarialist can and cannot do, I offer four examples of consultations performed for previous clients (2.1-2.4) and one (2.5) which was designed, but not carried out.


### *Disclaimers:*

Before proceeding to these examples, however, I must issue the following three disclaimers, the first two adapted in paraphrase from the **Exposure Draft of October 15, 1999, International Actuarial Association**, and the third, a caveat suggested by my counsel as standard practice:

--**Principle 3.5.** Avoidance of Failure: For most risk-management estimates with specified success criteria, there is a set of parameters such that a combination of values of the probabilistic criteria reduces the failure probability, as estimated by a valid actuarial model, to below a specified positive level.

--**Principle 3.6.** Degree of Actuarial Soundness: For most risk-management estimates, there is a set of parameters such that a combination of values produces a degree of actuarial soundness, as estimated by a valid actuarial model, that exceeds a specified level less than one.

--**Caveat:**

The examples which follow are intended solely to illustrate prior practice, and are not intended for use in any way, shape or form in the creation of plans or dreams by readers of this prospectus. In light of **Principles 3.5 and 3.6** *supra*, any reader who attempts to use directly, or to extrapolate from, said examples, does so at his or her own risk. In that event, **Actuarialist Life Solutions, Inc.**[tm] shall incur no legal liability whatsoever. In other words, don't try these in your own home or office!

**Example 2.1**. A 62-year old, six-foot tall, physically fit, diet-and-exercise-conscious, highly successful, black male advertising executive in excellent health, aside from very mild age-related scholiosis  and a history of hypertension and diabetes on the maternal branch, asked whether the Norfolk pine in his living room, currently 5'10" high and just sprouting its newest layer, will outgrow him.

***client's life expectancy*** (factored for likelihood of continued good health and for median life expectancy for African-American males age 62, 84.4): 85.39

**mean growth rate of Norfolk pines:** one layer every 1.17 years

**mean height of each layer of this particular tree:** four inches (4")*

*Strictly speaking, this number, 4", refers to the height of the section of the tree's stem between all produced, but not necessarily remaining, layers, since lower layers tend to fall off, especially in unhealthy trees, such as those which have been traumatized by events like ceiling collapse.

**actuarialistic assessment of likelihood of pine outpacing man:** barring unforeseen disease of, or accident to, tree, as close to certain as anything in this world can be.

**advice to client:** Count on it.

**comment:** In one way, this consultation was anomalous, since the client appeared to seek the information for no purpose other than some obscure mental or emotional satisfaction

**Example 2.2.**  A client in the 98th percentile for wealth, but with no other relevant demographic characteristics, asked me to determine the likelihood that the marriage of his daughter and only child (white, Episcopalian, age 20) to an immigrant from a war-torn African nation on his last year in the U.S. on a student visa (black, Baptist/animist, age ?27) will end in divorce, and, if so, the likelihood that this divorce will occur before or after the couple has produced a child or children.

**divorce rate from American wives for all males of this man's nationality (i.e., "tribe") on student visas in U.S.**

data unavailable

**divorce rate from American wives for all males from this man's country on student visas in U.S.**

27% (est. margin of error: 12%)

*mean duration of all terminated marriages:* 5.6 years (est. margin of error: 12%)

*mean time elapsed between marriage and production of (first) child in all terminated marriages:*

2.6 years (est. margin of error: 12 %)


*other relevant data:* the client has, himself, been divorced six times; his daughter's mother, twice; 87% of all members of the client's family have been divorced at least once, as have 63% of all members of his daughter's mother's family; in 94% of all divorces on both sides, an average of 2.4 children were produced prior to divorce and, in only 0.73 per cent, no children.

*advice to client:* The worst-case scenario (divorce after the production of a child or children) seems virtually certain. Deal.

*caveat to client:* [See **Principle 3.6. Degree of Actuarial Soundness (*supra*)**]. On the 0-1 scale, this prediction achieves only 0.347. To approach 0.750, the generally acceptable level of soundness in cases such as these, where the human factors are, alas, somewhat indeterminate, one would have to garner information relevant to at least two further *random variables:* cultural attitudes toward marriage and divorce within the groom's particular nationality, and divorce rates within both the groom's nuclear and extended families. Although obtaining both sets of information would be possible, the task would require at least two subcontractors: a private investigator within, or with access to, the groom's home country; and an anthropologist (cultural) cognizant of patterns of marriage and divorce within the groom's nationality. After a short deliberation, the client decided not to sign a second contract for these additional services. Quote: "No, that's okay, I get the picture."


**Example 2.3.** A farmer (truck and dairy) who depends for a significant proportion of his income on an elaborate, well-maintained farm stand which is situated directly beside the road just to the left of his large (3000 cubic-foot) barn asked for a cursory (i.e. inexpensive) study of whether he should repaint the sides and back of the barn as well as the front. It was a given that the barn needed painting. It was also a given that the *degree of actuarial soundness* he could expect from this study would be commensurate with the cost. In other words, the *stochastic model*, in this case, would be by no means *deterministic*.

*principal determinant* (I): comparison of sales volumes at farm stands proximate to buildings which are painted, unpainted, and partially painted. The ratio is I to .4 to .7.

*principal determinant* (2): cost of painting ($1700) and of partially painting ($950)* said barn.

*Given that the farmer has no children or other relatives residing in the area from whom he might extract free or barter labor, and given that both he and his wife "already have our hands full," $1700/$950 were the (sole) estimates for the job, as provided by two young, moderately experienced local men who are reputed to be honest, capable, and in possession of all necessary equipment.

*actuarialistic estimate:* the most cost-effective solution would be to paint only the front of the barn plus the side visible from the stand (the left side, from the vantage of the road and the entrance to the stand). Fortunately, the other (right) side faces an impenetrable grove of alders. It was also estimated (by intuition) that almost no customers who happen to wander around behind the barn to "sightsee" are likely to be deterred by the unpainted back of the barn from purchasing the produce, dairy products, jams and baked goods for which this farm stand is renowned.

*advice to client:* Get the boys out there before the weather (fair and cool) and the season (late-August) turn.

***conclusion:*** This was one of my favorite consultations. Since the barn was (partially) repainted two years ago,[**] sales from the stand, rather than declining, have actually increased 1.7% p.a.[***] Furthermore, since my own country house is located in the vicinity (2.8 miles) of the farm, I was pleased to waive my fee in favor of three summers' supply of "any and all products sold at ----Farms which can reasonably be construed as meeting the normal needs of a bachelor and temperate eater." In line with the **Caveat (Section 2. Introductory)**, however, readers of this prospectus should instantly disabuse themselves of any notion they may have conceived to the effect that my services could ever again be obtained on anything but a strictly cash basis. (See **Section 3. Fee Structure,** below.)


[**] actually costing, in the event, $936.28, or $13.72 below estimate.

[***]Professional standards compel me to point out, however, that unexamined ***random variables*** render absurd any assertion of a causal relationship between the paint job and the increase in sales.


**Example 2.4.** A seventy-one year-old woman (white, in excellent health) asked me to determine whether she will have time to knit a sweater for her unborn grandchild before either she (the grandmother) dies or the world ends.

*client's remaining life expectancy:* 13.4 years

***minimal "life expectancy" for Earth:*** 46 years.[****]

[****] Our best available estimate for the end of the world comes from the emerging science of econophysics, a movement among physicists which models economic systems using techniques and concepts initially developed to analyze the out-of-equilibrium dynamics of complex systems. Econophysicists have recently confirmed Sir Isaac Newton's famous Bible-based estimate that

the world will end c.2050. The corroborating estimate is based upon a singular convergence of many long-term demographic, economic and financial series.

My own interest in econophysics dates from shortly after the severance of my corporate affiliation. Incidentally, econophysicists also predicted that the Nikkei would rise 50% in 1990 (it "only" rose 49%), and they have recently predicted that the U.K. housing bubble will burst no later than 2004.

*client's projected time frame for project:* 6-18 months

*additional factor significantly impacting actuarialistic assessment of project's coming to fruition:* Over the past two years, the client's daughter, 34, and the daughter's live-in "other" (male, 31) have mentioned with increasing frequency their desire to produce a child "soon."

*advice to client:* Pick a pattern, buy the wool. The "baby" will be in his/her forties by the time the world ends, by which time he/she will have outgrown this and, presumably, many other sweaters.

**Example 2.5.** A 31 year-old woman wished to discover the likelihood that her neutered eight year-old Tom cat will attack the man who has been her lover for one month, while the man is sleeping. The cat has already inflicted several superficial scratches and one small bite while the man was awake.

*No further data available**

*This consultation did not occur. Not that the question was by any means unanswerable, but in order to establish adequate **random variables** ( i.e., to assign numerical values to the likelihood of attacks of various severity and of a non-attack), and subsequently to quantify all **probabilistic outcomes** (i.e., to assign a number between zero and one to the likelihood of attacks of various severity and of a non-attack), I estimated 20 hours of work at my usual fee of $180 per hour (see Section 3, below), whereupon the client decided not to proceed. In my own defense, let me explain that the ***random variables*** for this study would have been complex and subtle: for example, previous behavior by the cat toward prior boyfriends and any others who had been perceived (presumably) as rivals for the client's affection; plus the time frame of attack patterns by cats —to wit, ***longitudinal data*** concerning the increase or decrease of jealousy-aggression behavior among cats of various ages and sub-species -- if such data even exist.

As a courtesy, and in order to effect closure, I suggested to this non-client the expedient of locking the cat in an empty room at such times as said boyfriend is on the premises, with the caveat that she not choose the bathroom, in case the boyfriend should happen to get up in the night.

### 3. Fee Structure (see attached pamphlet)
### I.  Conclusion.

**On a personal note...** suffice it to say that, since my private life is virtually synonymous with my professional one, I am now happy. Rashly ignoring any and all projected health factors and all projected local, national, continental, planetary or cosmic disasters, whether induced by humans or so-called acts of God, I expect to remain same (happy) for 44.4 more years***** (based upon current life expectancy for 32 year-old white males in the U.S.).


***** which, I note --not without a certain ambivalence-- would bring me to A.D./C.E. 2048.


### The End

FOR A CHANGE of pace, and returning to factual ground, here is another tidbit from my family memoir, the conclusion to a section in which two of my widowed Grandma's sons-in-law bicker over how long she should be allowed to stay in each of their homes.

## A Note in the Interests of Equity

I CANNOT REMEMBER anyone ever having suggested that our long sojourns at my grandparents' house be credited against the account of Grandma's subsequent visits to us. The bottom line would have been, to use one of my mom's favorite adjectives, "interesting."

But never mind. By now, I am the family's principal surviving earthly accountant.

# II. BOOKS

"Reading maketh a full man."
–Francis Bacon[3]


IN A SENSE, every writer is an accountant. Not to mention how much I write about money. To wit: consider another story, also cut from whole cloth, about a third actuary, and about a different kind of reckoning. Understandably, many Gravy-ites, myself included, are also addicted to books. With the aid of our thick glasses, or laser-renewed lenses, we pore over thrillers, plough through Trollope, reread Tolstoy. We dominate the ranks of Lincoln buffs, Hitler buffs, Peloponnesian and Civil War buffs—everything buffs. Paul Wolf, a Dante acolyte, is a prime example.


## Dante's Way

## (Sul Percorso Di Dante)


UNTIL MY "RETIREMENT" thirteen years ago, I enjoyed a successful career as an actuary. Concurrently, I enjoyed an avocation as an amateur Dante[4] scholar, an avocation I have since

---

[3] Frances Bacon, "Of Studies," The Essayes or Counsels, Ciuill and Morall, of Francis Lo. Verulam, Viscount St. Alban (London, 1625), https://andromeda.rutgers.edu/~jlynch/Texts/studies.html

[4] All Dante quotations are from *The Inferno, Purgatorio* or *Paradiso* (transl. Robert & Jean Hollander, Random House, Anchor Books, 2000, 2004, 2008). The author wishes to point out that his narrator provides his

had more time to indulge. In fact, I am a charter member of the Metropolitan Alighieri Dante Society (MADS).

Here are a few details from the life and work of the Master that are germane to my story:

Dante commences his poetic journey of revenge and redemption in the throes of a mid-life crisis:

> *Nel mezzo del cammin di nostra vita*
> *mi ritrovai per una selva oscura*[5]

Or:

> In the midst of life's journey,
> I found myself lost in a dark wood.

By the time he began his masterwork, *Divina Commedia*, he was languishing in exile:

> *Tu proverai sì come sa di sale*
> *lo pane altrui, e come è duro calle*
> *lo scendere e 'l salir per l'altrui scale.*[6]

As the proverb goes, how salty the bread
in another man's house,

---

own translations, sometimes also deviating from the critical commentary of the Hollanders.

[5] (*Inf.* I.1-2)

[6] (*Par.* 17.55-60)

how steep the stairs!

The principle of revenge in *Inferno*, the first of the three books that comprise the *Commedia,* is called *contrapasso*: i.e., the punishment mirrors the crime. Yet the actual punishments that are meted out are often harsher, or less harsh, than the sinners would appear to deserve, even by the standards of early Fourteenth Century Italy. In many cases, Dante's own loyalties, passions, and quirks richly dye the *contrapassi,* as do the sinners' motives, virtues, and emotions.

Take the "outing" of his beloved teacher, Brunetto Latini, who languishes in the Seventh Circle, reserved for those who have sinned against nature. This particular judgment is tempered in several ways. Looking down from a ridge above the one on which Brunetto must endlessly walk and burn, the contrapasso for "cruising," the pupil expresses his respect:

> *Io non osava scender de la strada*
> *per andar par di lui; ma 'l capo chino*
> *tenea com' uom che reverente vada.*

> 'Though I dared not leave the upper path
> to walk the lower one with him, I kept
> my head bowed, as one who walks in reverence.[7]

After prophesying his visitor's future woes, the political feuds that will drive him into exile, Brunetto alludes vaguely to his own sin:

---

[7] *Inf.* 15.43-45

*In somma sappi che tutti fur cherci*
*e literati grandi e di gran fama,*
*d'un peccato medesmo al mondo lerci.*[8]


In sum, note that they were all clergy
or renowned scholars, befouled on earth by a single sin.


Note, too, the implicit boastfulness of "*literati grandi.*"
Brunetto further mutes his transgressions by graphically dissociating them from those committed by other gay men, including a sinner in the employ of Dante's archenemy, the "servant of servants," Pope Boniface VIII:

...e vidervi
s'avessi avuto di tal tigna brama,

colui potei che dal servo de' service
fu transmutato d'Arno in Bacchiglione,
dove lascio li mal protesi nervi.[9]

...And if you had shown
a hankering for such filth, you might have seen

the one transferred by that servant of servants
from the Arno to the Bacchiglione,
where his sin-stretched organ finally expired.

---

[8] *Inf.* 15.106-08
[9] *Inf.* 15.110-14

*In somma*, one might say, *Inferno* is the work of an angry man who, having lost his way in life, is groping for truth and justice. But, even so, it is the prevailing malice (e.g. the incidental jabs at Boniface and his minion) that has endeared the book to seven centuries of readers—myself included. In my case, a further reason the book speaks to me may be that, like the poet, I seem to have lost my way, and taken solace in revenge, though closer to the end of life than to the middle.

As another aside that I hope will prove illuminating (we old men are garrulous), let me recall Dostoevsky's Underground Man. Quoting from memory this time, and in my own loose translation, "I am a sick and spiteful man. I think my liver may be diseased." That's me, except for the liver. Mine is fine, which is more than can be said for some of my other body parts.

❖ ❖ ❖

WHO AM I, then? By name, Paul Wolf, I am an octogenarian whose years in exile on the Island of Old Age (increasingly populous, nowadays) are about to end. My life was not, of course, always so. As mentioned, I spent my working years as an actuary. My single employer for more than four decades was what is called a "super-cat" reinsurance company. Specifically, my job was to use stochastic calculus, a branch of mathematics, to calculate the odds and costs of likely natural disasters, and to help my masters determine the rates at which they could very profitably reinsure companies that sold primary insurance against these disasters.

Over all these years, and especially near the end, with the advent of severe climate change, there had certainly been no shortage of catastrophes. But, contrary to popular opinion, the most successful super-cat reinsurance companies make *more* money when catastrophes proliferate—if they have good actuaries, that is, not to mention large capital reserves, or, as a contemporary vulgarism puts it, "deep pockets." (Which is, strictly speaking, a dental term. I know about those from personal experience. The treatment is excruciating.)

Speaking of "deep pockets," as a highly competent senior employee, I was amply rewarded. Over the years, I was able to amass savings which, invested wisely, of course, would have enabled me to live very comfortably in retirement. But, owing to a major setback, what I came to desire more than money was to make those who had offended me live very *un*comfortably. Not as uncomfortably, perhaps, as Dante's souls in Hell, but very uncomfortably. Actually (or, if you a devotee of *paronomasia*, or puns, actuarially), it was my own masters against whom my wrath was directed. Although I hope you will agree that I had good cause, and that the plans for my revenge were clever, there is a strong probability that these plans are about to come to an end that is… catastrophic.

* * *

THE PRECIPITATING INCIDENT took place at 9:15 a.m., thirteen years, two months, and four days ago. This, coincidentally or not, is the same time of day that I now sit here at my keyboard. Without any notice, whatsoever, I was summoned to the Personnel Director's office.

I knew what was coming. First, my workload had been steadily increasing for sixty-three months, as my greedy employers relentlessly downsized my department. Until four months before my summons, two survivors, both of us very senior, had been doing the work previously done by five, then four, then three. Two months after that, my co-survivor, a highly competent woman about ten years younger than I (i.e. in her early 60s), also disappeared. The next morning, a bright young thing was already ensconced at her predecessor's desk, sharpening multitudinous virgin pencils. (We still used them in our "game.")

I was introduced to the new employee by the office manager, who directed me to "show this newbie the ropes."

"Newbie." Yet another neologism. And never mind the nautical cliché. Don't you love what is happening to the mother tongue? (Or is it, by now, the "parental" tongue?) Not that I am a prescriptive grammarian, someone, that is, who still believes English should assume the ostrich position, but the current rate of change is ridiculous. If languages were motor vehicles, there would be a massive pile-up on the Highway of Discourse.

At any rate, for me, "showing the ropes" was, to mix the metaphor, the handwriting on the wall. My own meeting with the new Personnel Director took place six weeks later. This would be the first time I had met her ("Laid eyes on her" sounds faintly salacious.)

"Hello, Paul," said the smooth-faced, forty-something African-American woman, offering me a firm handshake. "I have good news and bad news for you today."

As usual, the company had covered its bases, or its backside: a female of color, no less, in middle management. As for her "good news and bad news," we used to call such phrases "seesaw clichés," other examples being "hale and hearty," and "fat and forty." Whether hale or hearty, the new P.D., though forty, was anything but fat. *Au contraire*, she looked very trim in her black "power" suit (most definitely not a "Black Power" suit). Her empathic smile could have illuminated the Empire State building. Were her teeth capped, or did she have good dental genes?

To skip the bulk of our short conversation—a monologue, really, interspersed with a few grunts from me—the good news was that my parachute would be quite generous, about 18-karat. The bad news was obvious.

* * *

LESS OBVIOUS WAS the contrapasso I devised. About a month after my "termination" (not starring Arnold Schwarzenegger), I began to set a plan in motion. I was surprised to discover how easy it would be to get even with those ingrates, my ex-employers.

(Not) to divulge trade secrets, but I realized the firing process had been uncharacteristically sloppy. Yes, they had made me sign some forms: a guarantee of non-disclosure of proprietary methods; abdication of the right to work for competitors (with a long list of rivals, plus "any others"); a pledge not to contact any of the firm's other employees, past or present; and so forth. As most people know, forms like these carry varying amounts of legal weight, from zero, to "not if you have a decent lawyer." The only one that counted, the stricture against contact with other employees, could have been demolished in court by a summer intern. But, as I already realized, if the scheme I was about to undertake misfired, I might need not a lawyer, but an undertaker.

Even more remiss, perhaps, was the company's failure to change the locks. To make a long story short (I know, this one is already 1,650 words and counting), I decided to contact my two immediate predecessors on the chopping block. As Google informed me, both were still among the living, and for a small fee, I obtained their current home and e-mail addresses. Both of these good folks, I hoped, might well harbor simmering grudges against the firm.

Via text message, I suggested we get together at a café equidistant from our three domiciles, to discuss "a matter of mutual interest." Vagueness was best. Let them think I wanted to start a new business, or something. Neither did I add, "for old time's sake," which would have been patently disingenuous, since, as colleagues, we had always hunkered down in the rich data of our separate projects. Within a few minutes, affirmative replies were forthcoming.

The next morning, at 10:30 sharp, we were ensconced at a corner table of the café, with baked goods and beverages of choice (hot, since it was February) in front of us. After minimal pleasantries, I opened the proceedings with a prepared grabber: "I don't know about you two, but the company doesn't seem to have bothered to cancel my access." Their startled expressions told me I already had them on the hook. Although neither had touched their food or drink, they were practically salivating with curiosity.

"This is how I know. At the end of my termination interview, the P.D.—a new one, possibly after your time— informed me that my password would be invalidated in one hour. It was true, I checked. But, the other day, for some reason, I decided to try an old password, which I had temporarily lost ten years ago. Apparently, they had neglected to cancel that one, since lo and behold, it still works. Maybe, they were careless because they assumed my big severance bonus would guarantee undying loyalty. Ha! And there's more."

By now, Roger Mott, a big, red-faced man who must have been approaching seventy, and who obviously loved his food, was frozen, open-mouthed, with his fork poised in midair, a piece of *baba au rhum* dangling precariously from a single tine.

"Of course, even if they had tried to take proper precautions, they would still have had security issues, things they couldn't have guarded against. You know, it's not like, when they canned us, they forced us to eat lotus blossoms, to make us forget how the statistical models worked. I mean, we were the ones who *designed* those models, and the ones who wielded them all those years to make the firm filthy rich. But look at it from their point of view. What were they supposed to do, trade in good models for new, inferior ones?"

Estelle Saperstein, the third person at the table, and my immediate predecessor on the chopping block, was a tall, thin woman in her early seventies, about my age. Estelle had been *magna cum laude* with a double degree in math and physics from someplace good—Stanford, I think. As I paused for effect, she was apparently unaware that she was stirring her latté with her right index finger. Either the latté was no longer hot, or she was.

Still, cautiously, I nattered on. "Any hypothetical former employee still in possession of an active password, and who knew how to work the models, could either alter data in ways that severely reduced the firm's profits or, if said person preferred, partake of their assets." I suppressed an impulse to grin or to wink.

"But that password, Mr. Wolf," objected hardheaded Estelle, "must only be operative in the company's internal network. Your putative hacker would need access to the office computers. Didn't they ask you to return your keys? Or do you have old keys, too?" When a serious woman like Estelle makes a lame joke like that, you can tell she is in the throes of some overwhelming passion—in this case, revenge and/or greed. I knew she was on board.

"Call me 'Paul,' please, Estelle. The old password works in my apartment, on my personal laptop."

"Wow, a live p-word," cried Roger Mott, flipping the piece of baba home. "I never even thought of trying mine."

"Why should you have, Roger?" I replied. "An honest, loyal fellow like yourself? And I bet *you're* so honest," I said to Estelle, "that you never thought of trying yours, either. Besides, it doesn't matter whether your passwords work. Mine does." Estelle's finger had stopped stirring her latté, but it was still extended, as if she were checking the wind.

"Which caper should it be?" asked Roger, devouring the rest of his pastry in two huge bites. "Rob them blind, or make the business crash?" He was obviously a zealot.

"Why does it have to be either-or?" asked Estelle mildly.

"O, ho! You took the words right out of my mouth," I said, which was true. "But let's drink up, before our beverages get cold."

"May I propose a toast?" suggested Estelle, who now wore a loopy, myopic grin. "To larceny," she whispered.

"To *grand* larceny," Roger.also whispered.

We drank to that, and agreed to meet again, two days later, same time, same place, which Roger dubbed "the War Room." Meanwhile, I would set in motion the process of extracting company data. After I had paid the check, tip included, we shook hands and went our separate ways.

Let me underline the fact that, at each stage of my pitch, I had kept a weather eye out. If either of my co-terminatees had shown the faintest signs of panic or moral umbrage, I would have shut my piehole fast, except for eating the apple pie I had ordered, which turned out to contain too much cinnamon, anyway.

In the event, I *should* have shut my P.H. Thirteen years later, this is no longer an option. So what? In for a dollar, in for…damnation. But that, as a witty college professor of mine once quipped, is "putting Descartes before Ho-race" (which he pronounced with a French accent, making it sound like "horse").

I proceeded in logical order. To oversimplify, I would hardly have waited to rob the company until I had bankrupted them. Without getting too technical (since I assume the reader is not using this story as a sleeping pill), here are a few salient details. I should point out, in passing, that by the time the three of us reconvened, my larcenous maneuvers were already well under way. When I laid out the plan, far from demurring, Roger and Estelle seemed mesmerized.


**Fleecing the Firm:** Using pseudonyms, and what are called "margin accounts" (which basically means buying things with other people's money), in the course of a few months, with credits from several brokerage houses, we made about 100 separate purchases of company stock, each between 50 and 300 shares. We then sold all the shares at their current price (high). A few months later, after we had caused the stock to plummet (see *infra*), we re-paid the brokers in re-purchased shares (low).

Need I add that these machinations involved unnumbered Swiss accounts? All told, we probably netted about 57.36 million dollars. "Probably"? "About"? These qualifications stem from the fact that the purloined amounts are stated in 2005-dollar values. Of course, being a man of my word, my own share was a paltry 19-plus.

The larceny entailed one further wrinkle. We transferred our profits to the banks through a tortuous trail of fictitious entities, so that anyone who smelled a rat would have had to bait the trap and chase the rodent for months, through places to which the chaser could not have gained access. If that sounds murky, it was. The best way to understand it is to think of money laundering, the sort of thing you have undoubtedly read about in connection with spy rings and drug cartels.

Timing, as I said, was crucial. Immediately after our final purchase, we began the demolition phase.

**Deep-Sixing the Corporate Vessel:** This phase was also carried out by means of a single process, which involved something called "float."[10] A bit more arcane than margin accounts, float is money set aside to meet anticipated claims. Normally (and don't forget, Roger, Estelle, and I wrote the book), the firm would invest according to the size of estimated future claims, and their timeframe: the shorter the timeframe (called "short-tail float," or STF), the more conservative the investments. Our tactic now was

---

[10] "What Does 'Float' Mean," *The Business Dictionary*, 2019, www.businessdictinary.com/definition/float,html.

to transfer a large percentage of the company's STF into dubious instruments, such as junk bonds and penny stocks. For long-term float, or LTF, we transferred funds from the current, more speculative instruments into high-quality, low-yield bonds, mostly ten-to-thirty-year Treasury notes.

How, you ask, were we able to hide these manipulations[11] from the company's current actuaries, not to mention its auditors? Dodging the latter, a highly competent bunch, was easy: we performed our statistical prestidigitations in the weeks *right before* the annual audit. And let me tell you, that audit was a sight to behold. More than half of it was in **BOLDFACE CAPS**.

The way we fooled the actuaries falls under the heading, So Technical As To Be Soporific. (*Caveat, lector.* You can skip this paragraph.) As I just mentioned, the general strategy was to reverse the normal pattern of investments. The money transfers were made in the names of about thirty low-level company employees, and through a series of fictitious entities. By the time the actuaries could trace the paper trail, the damage had been done, apparently by the same people who cleaned their toilets and emptied their wastebaskets. A secondary pleasure was our knowledge that, when we had still been with the Department, chicanery like this would have been detected almost immediately, and ruthlessly staunched.

Please note that the bear market in U.S. stocks did not begin until 2007, whereas the operations of The Three Marketeers ended in mid-2006. In terms of the market collapse, we were minnows, although, regrettably, the minnows' revenge occasioned extensive collateral damage, such as the bankruptcy of several insurance companies, with the concomitant loss of thousands of jobs. To make our omelet, yes, we broke a lot of innocent eggs. For that, I am truly sorry, but those eggs will be happy to learn

---

[11]www.investopedia.com/university/shortselling/shortselling1.asp

that I, at least, am about to undergo a severe, if belated, punishment.

* * *

IT IS TIME to explain the hints I have been dropping like breadcrumbs about the demise of my scheme. About three or four weeks ago, one of my co-conspirators defected. And this, thirteen years after having gratefully acknowledged the receipt of some nineteen million dollars. In true cowardly fashion, she (yes, Estelle) confessed her defection via text message. By resorting to this, the most impersonal and pusillanimous mode of communication, she avoided facing my wrath, face-to-face:

Estelle: *hi p. scnd thghts 2 rsky cnt me out. srry e*

For the text-illiterate: "Hi, Paul. Second thoughts. Too risky. Count me out. Sorry, Estelle."

"Too risky?" After thirteen years? To which circle of Hell should such a disingenuous coward and ingrate be consigned? Too angry to argue, or even to reply, I realized I had a huge problem. Why had I ever thought I needed partners? I hate to admit it, but the reason may have been as simple as an old, newly unemployed man's loneliness. Well, soon enough, I would have plenty of company—kindred souls, too.

I mulled my options:

1. Murder the woman in some cruel, Dantean fashion. Not me. Grand Larceny is one thing, but…I wonder if, aside from the heat of battle, Dante ever murdered anyone.

2. Try to buy her silence with an additional tranche from my ill-gotten gains. As I said, my principal motive had been revenge, not greed.

But before I could decide to bribe Estelle, another shoe—the second, third? —fell. A few days after her perfidious text message, I received a registered letter from the New York State Attorney General's Office, summoning me to appear before the Department of Financial Services, Insurance Division, at such-and-such an hour, such-and-such a date, in six weeks' time. Although the letter outlined a complex process by which I could request a postponement, what would have been the point? Conceivably, of course, the summons could have been triggered by something I had done while I was at the firm. Sure. It could also have been sent by hackers from Mars.

Yesterday morning, I saw something that made it certain the summons was, indeed, related to my peculations. A small death notice in the Paper of Record told me that Estelle Saperstein had passed at the age of 83 (a widow, without progeny). So much for bribing (or murdering) this woman. Presumably, her long-harbored remorse had led to an eleventh-hour decision to spill the beans, including chapter-and-verse of the M.O. I had outlined to her and Roger Mott at the café that fateful morning thirteen years ago. Estelle had made a deathbed confession of *my* crimes.

What of Roger? A quick phone call, on the pretext of asking whether he had read Estelle's death notice, revealed that, for whatever reason (and who cares?), Estelle had not ratted him out. A quick calculation told me that only two realistic options remained: federal prison or Dante.

Option One: I could spend my remaining days making license plates for twelve cents an hour.

Option Two: I could spend forever being torn limb from limb in the Second Ring of Circle Seven, the Violent Against Themselves.

This particular contrapasso is even more convoluted than most. As Dante learns from one of the damned, when a suicide's soul flees his despised body, the body is flung into a wood, where it metamorphoses into a thicket, the leaves of which the Harpies eat, inflicting excruciating pain. Since the thicket is a perennial, of sorts, the torture is unending. After Judgment Day, when the soul descends to reclaim its body, an even more exquisite wrinkle kicks in. (I know, I know, a mixed metaphor.)

> *...ma non pero ch'alcuna sen rivesta,*
> *che non e giuasto aver cio ch'om si toglie.*

> *Que le straschinermo, e per la mesta*
> *selva seranno I nostril corpi appesi,*
> *ciascuno al prun de l'ombra sua molesta.*[12]

> ...But it would be unjust were we again
> to clad ourselves in the flesh looted from our own souls.

> So here we shall drag it, and in this gloomy wood
> will our bodies hang, each one
> on the thorn bush of its painful soul.

*Caro lettore* (Dear Reader), which punishment would you have chosen? Prison, I assume? But, as always, I am more curious than prudent. So I will end this long account by noting that I am about to proceed to the bathroom, where, among my panoply of medicaments is a paracetamol compound reserved for just such an eventuality as this.

Don't be shocked. Keep in mind that, were I to expire from natural causes in prison, I might meet the even more unspeakable fate of being consigned to the Ninth, and lowest, Circle, near the

---

[12] *Inf.* 13.104-08

very bottom of which suffer those who have betrayed their masters. But let's not go there.

**SOURCES.**

Technical details about re-insurance: http://alephblog.com/2014/07/23/understanding-insurance-float/

https://www.investopedia.com/university/shortselling/shortselling1.asp

Berkshire-Hathaway Annual Report, 2017: www.berkshirehathaway.com/2017ar/2017ar.pdf

**The End**

DID YOU NOTICE when Paul Wolf described old age as an island? "Gravy Island" has a nice ring to it. Speaking of which:

## Marooned on the Desert Isle of Age...

...where the diet is strictly limited (you'd kill for a scotch or a cheeseburger); you can never get your bearings; the routine never varies; one tires, even, of the clear blue sky—and never mind the sun, which sears your eyeballs and constitutes (*pace* the single palm tree) the ideal incubator of metastatic melanomas (you left your hat in the lifeboat)

...where shores are washed by treacherous undercurrents, and the clear green waters are infested with grinning sharks (you used to love to swim)

...where one longs for any company: a tedious nephew, dotty stranger, an enemy or two, or even (God forbid) a pontificating professor, pontifical evangelical, or gassy politician

...where, however, the litany of complaint remains: nagging aches, sagging skin, fussy bladder, flaccid limbs, shrinking muscles, wrinkles, wens; and the fact that, even when you had a phone, the children never called.

Like Wolf, my unnamed alter-ego in the next story is a bibliophile, although the writer to whom he is devoted is less well known than Dante.

# The Printed Word

READERS OF PRINTED books on the subway are becoming as scarce as hen's teeth. So, the other day, when, among all the texters, shoppers, gamers, and trawlers, I spotted one (a reader, that is), I experienced what former Fed Chairman Alan Greenspan famously called "irrational exuberance." As for the book he was reading, to judge from its handsome, but discreet, cover, it looked like one of those trade-paperback editions of interesting novels from around the globe, which are issued, for the most part, by European houses. In short, it looked *literary*. So did the reader. A tall, slender, bald man, he wore dark pants, a long-sleeved white shirt, no tie, pointy black European shoes, and small black-framed glasses.

From my seat diagonally across the aisle, I strained to read the cover, which was pointing in my direction. "Maybe he's the author," I thought, "and hopes I'll buy a copy." But the print, alas, was too small. If a gun had been held to my head, I might have made a random guess—say, Borislav M. Posner, *Life After Budapest.*

When the train reached my stop, I exited, as did the reader. Walking along the platform, I adjusted my pace to his. He now held the book at his side, where, thanks to the fickle gods of chance, the title might be legible. But since his gait caused the book to swing back and forth, the only way I could have read the title would have been to crouch down and swivel my head back and forth in time with his steps.

Since a man has his dignity, I gave up, and continued to my destination, a private library where I had a study room reserved. Like many people, I imagine, I work better when my day begins with a diversion. Need I say that I (too) am a writer? I was planning a new story, in which an actuary would inflict Dantean retribution on an insurance company for downsizing him.

After ninety minutes, and four or five aborted openings, it was time for either suicide or an early lunch. Since it was a mild May day, I walked west on 79th Street from the library to Central Park, where I sat down on a bench facing a verdant hill, and opened the paper bag containing my frugal meal: cheese, crackers, a little apple, and a bottle of water.

Did I call the gods of luck fickle? Who should I see, two benches to my left, but...? With a soft pretzel in one hand, in the other he held The Book, which he was still reading. This time, my curiosity was not to be thwarted. Repacking my lunch, I hurried over and pointed to the unoccupied half of his bench. "May I?"

Since there were several empty benches nearby, I worried that he might suspect me of a nefarious motive. But, with a smile, he said, in a smooth baritone, "Please."

I sat down and, for a few moments, we munched away in silence. Then, as casually as I could, I gestured to the book and said, "You know, I saw you reading that book on the subway, and I was..." My sentence was interrupted by a fit of coughing, caused by a crumb that had taken a wrong turn.

"Are you okay?"

Even in my distress, I noticed that he spoke with a faint accent. An amateur linguist, I surmised that he was a well-educated speaker of an East or West Slavic language (as opposed to South Slavic). The odds were, he was Russian or Polish, since those are the largest Slavic populations in the city.

"Drink some water," he suggested. It worked, and a loud moment of throat clearing ended the attack.

"Crumbs," I said.

"Allergy season."

"Anyway," gesturing to the book again, "I was curious about your book." He pointed the cover at me, and—no surprise—the print was in Cyrillic. Despite my layman's interest in linguistics, the only alphabet I can read is the Latin. My interlocutor's sly half-smile suggested he had shown me the cover as a practical joke.

"Would you like to know what it says?"

"Sure."

"*The Calculus of Alienation: Leo Perutz, A Life.* In Russian." Looking again, I saw that the cover image was of a pair of intertwined flowers, one red, the other white, at the base of a small bridge. "A genius," he declared. "Do you know his work?"

"I do. In fact, I think I even remember that image. It's from one of his novels, isn't it?" As I said this, I recognized it as a small outbreak of my abiding sin, intellectual pride.

Instead of being impressed, as I had expected, my interlocutor looked annoyed. "Very good." He sounded like a teacher condescending to a dull pupil. "But what I bet you didn't know is that this is the best biography of Perutz. Are you familiar with his life?"

"Wasn't he a Jew who lived in Prague and wrote in German? Like Kafka?"

"Yes, and no. Actually, he was born in Prague, in 1882, but moved to Vienna. Then, in 1938, he fled to Palestine, and in 1957, died at an Austrian spa. But we're neglecting our lunches." He took another bite from his pretzel, and I ate a bit more cheese and cracker, this time washing it down with a swig of water.

"He did write in German, didn't he?"

"Yes, of course, and the only other full-scale biography, to date, is also in German. I am preparing an English translation of this one, which I anticipate will be the definitive work for years to come." Was it my imagination, or did he seem to fluff himself up, like a preening bird?

"You know," I said, somehow chastened, "I think I'll reread Perutz." He nodded, and we lapsed into silent munching. After a minute or so, I consulted my phone. "I'm afraid I have to get back to work now," I lied. "I'll look for your book when it comes out."

The stranger extended a hand, but when I took it, he did not let go. His hand was dry and bony, and his handshake had an Ancient Mariner feeling. "I'd better tell you my name, then," he said, "because the title I mentioned is only a working title. I am Phillip Danilov, two 'l's,' then one."

"Pleased to meet you," I muttered, without disclosing my own name.

"This biography," he continued, finally releasing my hand, "focuses on the relationship between the two facets of Perutz's genius. He was also a mathematician, the creator of what is called the Perutz equation. Again, like Kafka, he worked for an insurance company, but in Perutz's case, as an actuary."

"That all sounds fascinating, Mr. Danilov. I'll certainly keep an eye out for your translation. Meanwhile, *Sposibo. Das vadanya.*" Since I was leaving, why not expend my meager supply of Russian?

"Bye, bye," he replied.

With that, I fled further into the park. When I looked back, Danilov was once again immersed in his reading, and biting into the last loop of his big pretzel. As I wandered over hill and dale, I had the sense that I was running away from something. My work? Him? Possibly adding to my unease was the fact that the story I was trying to start also featured an actuary, although, so far, at least, mine had nothing to do with Perutz.

After ten minutes of hurrying hither and yon, guilt nudged me back toward the library. To avoid the bench I had shared with

Danilov, I veered south, and exited the park at 76th Street. A few minutes later, I was back in my cozy workroom where, reluctant to waste any more time, I made a resolution that will be familiar to many readers: "Just one click."

Googling "Leo Perutz," I found a biographical summary[13] that went over much the same ground as Danilov and I had covered. The novels, I discovered, had been translated into several languages, including Russian. Of the numerous studies, however, including articles, dissertations, and books, most were in German, several each in French, Italian, and English, but not a single one in Russian. My personal favorite was an article by one "Josef Quack."

As is often the case, one click led to another. This time, I tried "Phillip Danilov." I found a few people with that name on Facebook, and quite a few Danilovs with other first names, but none of them sounded anything like my self-declared translator.

Finally, like a drunk trying to exit a bar in the wee hours, I vowed, "Just one more click," and searched "*The Calculus of Alienation: Leo Perutz, A Life.*" I got, of course, nothing. By then, I was too tired even to think of creative work, so I decided to read for a while.

The book in my backpack, *A Crown of Feathers*, was a collection of short fiction by another Jewish writer, Isaac Bashevis Singer (my namesake). Singer had written not in German, but in Yiddish, and had helped translate some of his own work into English. I continued with "The Magazine," a story describing a character named Zeinvel Gardiner's quixotic efforts, over many years, to start a small Yiddish literary magazine. Coming upon

---

[13] Edward James, "Science Fiction and Fantasy Writers in the Great War," 2014. https://fantastic-writers-and-the-great-war.com/the-writers/leo-perutz/

the sentence, "I should have given Zeinvel a flat no,"[14] I unconsciously inserted a combined Yiddish-ism and British-ism: "I should have given Zeinvel a flat, no?" Realizing I was too tired even to read, I lay down on the gray pebble carpeting of my workroom, and using my shoes as a pillow, gained instant access to sleep.

* * *

I DREAMT OF—who else?—Leo Perutz. Entering a dimly lit, cavernous room that smelled of dust and food, I found the author seated on one side of a long worktable, facing the door. With his glasses pushed up on his forehead, he was bent over a meal. Spoon poised, he was also apparently examining a bound manuscript, which he held in the other hand.

"Come in, Mr. Singer," he said in a soft tenor. Carefully, he placed the spoon on an empty spot on the cluttered table. Crossing the room, I saw by the light of two large candles, on either end of the table, that his meal, in a soup bowl, was some kind of thick, darkish substance, with dumplings peeping out, and herbs on top. Alongside the bowl was a large, half-full glass of dark red wine. Both the food and wine smelled delicious. He gestured to a chair across from his. "Please," he said.

"I apologize for disturbing your meal, sir." Edging around the table, I sat down.

"Would you care to join me?" He gestured to a room on his right, from which wafted the same inviting smells. "There's more of this on the stove in the kitchen. Feel free to help yourself."

---

[14] Singer, Isaac Bashevis, "The Magazine," transl. by the author and Laurie Colwin. In *A Crown of Feathers* (N.Y. Farrar, Strauss and Giraux, 1970, p.175). This story originally appeared in *The New Yorker.*

66

"It's kind of you to offer, sir, but I've already eaten." I had carried into my dream a feeling of fullness from my *al fresco* lunch. Recalling the flight from Phillip Danilov ("two 'l's,' then one"), I realized uneasily that I must have left the remains of the lunch on our bench.

"A glass of wine, then, perhaps? The bottle is also in the kitchen."

"Thanks again, sir. But I happen to be a beer drinker."

"Oh, ho. Are you familiar with the Staropromen brand?"

"It happens to be a favorite. My wife and I discovered it on a trip to Prague some years ago."

"I'm sorry I don't have any in the house, or I would certainly have offered you some. But...doctor's orders." He patted his stomach, making me wonder what kind of ailment allowed him to consume red wine—and what I now guessed to be blood pudding—but not beer. All I knew about the author's health was that he had suffered a bullet wound during World War One, and, decades later, died at a spa.

Perutz guided his plate over toward the spoon, placed the manuscript face down on a pile of books, and lowered his glasses. His magnified eyes gazed at me with benign expectancy.

"Well, then, Mr. Singer. What can I do for you?" He sounded like a shopkeeper.

In speeded-up dreamtime, I offered a circumstantial account of my encounter in the park, only slowing down when I reached the point of asking him about Philip Danilov's ostensible translation project. As I fumbled for words, he interrupted.

"And you would like to know whether to believe this man and his tale. I mean, you see a stranger reading on the subway, and then again, in a park. Because you are curious about his book, you go out of your way to make his acquaintance. He freely describes to you a supposed Russian biography which, when he has translated it to English, will supplant the current standard, Hans-Harald Muller's. Correct?"

"Correct."

"Having subsequently checked, you find no such Russian biography. So. What you would like me to tell you is this man's motive for inventing such a book, and trying to pass it off on you, a stranger. I think you said you were a writer, yourself, Mr. Singer?"

I hadn't said that, but in dreams people just seem to know things. "I am. And, yes, I wondered about his motives."

"Well, my friend," he said with a dry smile, leaning back in his chair, and folding his hands behind his head. "Glad to oblige. This man, Danilov, is in self-chosen exile from Putin's kleptocracy. Yes, he is a little mad, and yes, a bit of a fraud. He and his wife—no children—rent a small apartment in Brighton Beach, Brooklyn. But, like that character in Hawthorne—you must have read the story, the title of which eludes me—Mr. Danilov lives a double existence. To the knowledge of the wife, who works in the cafeteria of a large department store—Macy's, I think—he spends his days trudging around the city searching for suitable employment. In Russia, he was a mid-level clerk for a mining concern.

"Yes, this fellow is indeed a Russian. But, like many exiles, alas, he has developed an almost total amnesia for his native tongue. The only Russian word he can accurately remember is his own surname. His given name, dimly recalled, is 'Filip,' and his patronymic—forgotten—'Leonovich.' Which may be one reason he is fixated on me."

"What about the book?"

"The book he showed you is a fiction wrapped in a lie. Like most good lies, this one is not unrelated to truth. The book he carries around like a personal Bible is a copy of the Russian translation of perhaps my best-known novel, *Nachts unter der steinernen Brücke*, or *By Night Under the Stone Bridge*."

"Ah, ha! I thought I recognized the cover. This lie must be flattering to you, sir."

"Not really. Why should I be flattered by a weak attempt at a scam? Let me explain further." Glancing at his food, which had lost its pungency, Perutz continued talking.

"You see, my friend, among the elderly—especially widows and widowers who frequent those benches on the affluent eastern side of Central Park—are many who will hear him out. When he puts the bite on them, some might even subscribe a few dollars, or invite him to join them for a meal at a fancy restaurant."

"But why would they do that?"

"Who can say? Loneliness? Love of literature? A longing to get back into the swim, after dreary decades of retirement? Who knows?"

"I see."

"But even though you were so curious about Danilov's book, *you* didn't fall for the scam. Why not? Again, I can only guess. As a writer, you have a life—and, I presume, a wife? Or is she...?"

"No, thank god, and we have grown children and grandchildren."

"He must have misread you, then. Anyway, the scam is never much of a success, except that it keeps him talking, which may be his ultimate motive." With that, Perutz signaled the end of the discourse by moving his food back into place, eating a spoonful of pudding, and chasing it down with a sip of wine.

Why was I still less than satisfied with his explanation? "If you'll excuse me, sir," I blurted out, "I don't think that talking is his ultimate motive."

Perutz bestowed on me the warm smile of a teacher for a bright student. "All right," he said, then fell into silent thought for a moment. "At the root of his behavior may be what is called compartmentalization. This tendency lies behind much of what we all do. We create mental ghettoes. In the novel that Danilov carries around with him, Esther Meisl does just that, when she remains her husband, Mordecai's, devoted wife, even as she welcomes the ardent caresses of Emperor Rudolf."

Perutz shrugged. "We creative types are always trying to break out of these compartments, Mr. Singer, trying to connect them. I suppose Danilov's is an extreme case. Unable to remember his mother tongue, he pretends to be an expert Russian linguist who is endeavoring to break down the barrier between people interested in my work, and the so-called best book about it. As Saint John wisely said, 'In the beginning was the word.' For Danilov, the word is beginning, middle, and end."

Perutz laughed drily. "Well, my friend," he sighed, "I've subjected you to a long discourse. Perhaps I'm lonely, myself. But I shouldn't keep you from your work any longer." (Keep *me* from *my* work—*him*, from *his*, he meant.) I stood up to leave.

"Hmm," he said, half to himself, "I still wonder why he thought you might be a good prospect. Was it because you threw yourself in his way? Or are you, perhaps, just setting out to write something new and, hence, a bit lost in that limbo of fear and expectation so familiar to us all?"

I smiled and stood up. Again, Perutz gestured toward the kitchen, and again I became aware of the delicious odors wafting from that direction. There must have been a cauldron in there.

"No, thanks," I said, and pointed to the turned-over manuscript. "You wouldn't be procrastinating, yourself, would you, sir?"

With a barking laugh, he winked. I awakened on the hard floor of my library workroom, and, hurrying to the desk, woke up my laptop and, in a flurry, drafted the first paragraph of my story:

# Dante's Way
## (Sul Percorso Di Dante)

UNTIL MY "RETIREMENT" thirteen years ago, I enjoyed a successful career as an actuary. Concurrently, I enjoyed an avocation as an amateur Dante scholar, an avocation I have since had more time to indulge. In fact, I am a charter member of the Metropolitan Alighieri Dante Society (MADS).

## The End

FOR WHATEVER REASON, reading and scamming are often paired in my stories. In this next one, you may be hard pressed to say who scams whom.

## READER, I READ TO HIM

"Reader, I married him."[15]

## Part One

ONE EVENING (NOT dark, not stormy) about a month ago, I decided to read to my cat. Since I'm not completely crazy, I realized this was a quixotic idea. But since I always talk to Charles, anyway, reading aloud would give me something new to say. Besides, Charles is very smart. I mean, he once dragged the leash of his fellow pet—Muffin, a dog—over to me, when it was time to walk him (Muffin). He also has a habit of playfully ambushing the dog, who is three or four times his size. Each time Charles leaps out at him, Muffin looks as startled as he did the first time. Maybe he is playing, too.

"Charles, Charles, pss." The small black neutered male with the white blaze and white paws opened one green eye. He was curled up in his usual place at one end of the couch, opposite my armchair. Seeing that no food was in the offing and having had his fill of petting for the day, he closed the eye. But Muffin, a Golden Lab, immediately unfolded his large body from his dog bed in front of the couch and ambled over to me. Muffin is affectionate, even for a dog. This time, his normally kind and

---

[15] Bronte, Charlotte. *Jane Eyre*, (London, Penguin Classics, 2006) chapter 38.

alert expression looked as if he were consoling me for Charles's indifference. After I had thumped his side two or three times and scratched his forehead, Muffin returned to his bed.

It was time to read. Too lazy to walk over to the bookcase to find something suitable, I settled for the opening of a novel I was already reading. Clearing my throat, I began:

"When young Mark Robarts was leaving college, his father might well declare that all men began to say all good things to him, and to extol his fortune in that he had a son blessed with so excellent a disposition. This father was a physician living at Exeter."[16]

The passage produced the non-reaction I had anticipated from Charles. Actually, he twitched once or twice and looked annoyed. Muffin, of course, kept right on panting. Since it was a warm evening, his tongue also flapped, and his big brown dog eyes gazed ardently at me—and at the rest of the world. Of course, it was unlikely that either animal's non-reaction had much to do with Trollope, although, come to think of it, the non-reactions may have mirrored my own feeling that this writer is something of a plodder. In different ways, both of my pets have sensitive antennae, to use a metaphor that conflates insects with animals.

I probably should have stopped right there, but I stubbornly decided to push on. Isn't this what real scientists do? For instance, I once heard of a trick used by the Curator of Great Apes at a celebrated zoo. (I forget which one.) In order to stimulate a sluggish male to mate, he first tried projecting a pornographic black-and-white film, with human actors, onto the wall of the ape couple's cage: no reaction. Next, he tried images of apes mating: again, nothing. The third time, he tried human porn

---

[16] Trollope, Anthony. *Framley Parsonage* (New York, Harcourt, Brace and World, Inc.: 1962), I.

again, but this time in Technicolor. Bull's eye. The apes went, well, ape.

An interesting sidelight to this story is that the Curator himself was a burly, hairy man with long arms. Perhaps that helps explain his empathy. A mutual acquaintance also shared a rumor with me: when the unmarried forty-year old Curator was about to leave town for a conference, or something, he would always call his mother to tell her his itinerary. I'm not sure what, if anything, that has to do with the mating experiment.

Inspired by the Curator's success, I decided to go cat-centric. Like him, too, I would improvise. This time, I paraphrased the Trollope passage:

"When young Tabitha reached the age of seventeen weeks, Margaret Robarts realized that the time was fast approaching when the attractive feline would be crossing over from kittenhood to maturity. Stroking the cat under the chin, her indulgent mistress declared, 'You know, Tabby, one of these days, I'm going to have to get you spayed. But, first, I'd love for you to experience the joys of sex and motherhood. I know: I'll consult the vet.'

By then, Tabitha was purring like an expensive sports car right after a tune-up. Opening her eyes, she gazed at Margaret in a way that almost suggested she had understood her mistress's kind words."

Well, Tabitha (and Muffin) may have expressed interest in these shenanigans, but not Charles, who dozed on. Abandoning the experiment for the moment, I hoisted myself out of my chair and headed for the kitchen to make some popcorn. Of course, both pets now dogged (sorry) my heels, and treats were duly tendered. I never tease them about food.

I'm sure that, by now, Reader, you think I should have consigned my experiment to the scrap heap of bad ideas. Since I did not, let me justify myself, to a degree, by admitting that I'm a retired widower with few friends, one married daughter who is always busy, and not a single grandchild.

My faithful pets followed me back into the living room, and we resumed our positions. Fortified by a few mouthfuls of warm popcorn, I proceeded to Plan C. This time, I decided to paraphrase a passage from *Persian* Fire, another, more exciting book, which I had also been reading. I would add to the suspense by once again personalizing—felinizing—the passage. The original describes a small Spartan force preparing to face the Persian hordes at Plataea.

"Only the claws of **cats** like **Charles**, clotting the earth of Platea with the butchery of a blood-sacrifice, could possibly have secured the victory over the swarming hordes of **mice**. For those claws belonged to **cats** that had been steeled from birth to fight, to kill, and never to yield. Charging across the kitchen, **Charles** and the other **cats** smashed into the front line of **mice**."[17]

Looking up from the book, I saw Muffin gazing at me, as usual, with uncritical adoration. Of course, if *he* had been the subject of the experiment, I would have inserted *his* name and species into the narrative, but I doubt it would have made any difference. As for Charles, my emphatic reading appeared to have acted as a soporific: he was sleeping more deeply than usual, with a look of intense concentration on his face that suggested he was dreaming.

In hindsight, I'm not surprised by the failure of my experiment, which had one final, disastrous incarnation. In a way, however, the experiment was also a success. I'll give you a hint: do you remember what I said about the dog's leash and the ambushes?

Critiquing my third attempt, I felt I had been correct in tailoring the reading to my auditor, but that, intelligent though

---

[17] Holland, Tom. *Persian Fire* (New York, Anchor Books, 2005)35.

this auditor may have been, I had overestimated his capacity to relate to unfamiliar experience. After all, my house is so clean that I doubt Charles had ever so much as seen a mouse. Now I would try to come up with something that would require no such leap of imagination.

This called for a narrative created from whole cloth. Opening my smartphone, I began tapping away, and thirty minutes later, the passage was written. I leave it to you, Reader, to decide whether you could have done better.

"Once upon a time, there lived a widower with two pets, **a cat, Charles**, and a dog, Muffin. The man loved his pets dearly, affording them every possible comfort and pleasure. One evening, however, he awoke in his armchair to discover that neither animal was in its accustomed place. Where **Charles** usually lay, on the couch, was an empty indentation. Although the indentation was larger, Muffin's dog bed on the floor was similarly empty. Shifting his gaze to the French doors across the room, which had been left open to allow the entry of air on this warm evening, the man saw the curtains swaying in the breeze. Muffin and **Charles** had disappeared."

Having recited the passage, I looked up, hoping to see my dear cat gazing at me alertly. To my chagrin, however, I discovered something much worse than his previous indifference: not only was he gone, but so was Muffin. Rushing across to the open French doors and looking out, I was just in time to see, by the light of a full moon, the two animals scampering off toward the far end of the garden.

"Muffin. Charles. Sit!" For a moment, this worked. Both animals stopped in their tracks. Muffin looked back at me, awaiting further orders. But Charles, I could swear, winked, and then, with a single raucous "meow," leapt through the open door at the back of the garden and disappeared into the night.

* * *

AS I MENTIONED at the beginning, these events took place about a month ago. If Charles were less resourceful, I am certain he would have returned to his food source by now. And doesn't he know how much Muffin and I miss him? Every night, the poor dog keens for hours, while his poor master suffers in silence. Of course, I have posted notices all over the neighborhood, offering a large reward for Charles's return. God forbid, could he be. . .?

It has reached the point where I find myself praying for an extremely unlikely coincidence: that some other fool has taken in my wonderful cat and, at some point, will stumble upon the same disastrous idea I did. I cling to the hope that Charles's new master will find a story, and read it to him, about a runaway cat that, dearly missing his owner and fellow pet, determines to find his way back home. There must be some children's book where that happens.

## Part Two

AFTER PRAYER AND fantasy, I went through several other phases in trying to cope with Charles' disappearance. If you have ever mourned the death of a loved one, you will recognize them: denial (same as prayer?), rage (well, anger and touchiness), guilt (who had given him the idea of running away?), projection (perhaps his running off somehow echoed my own occasional urges to disappear), and, finally, acceptance. With the last phase, I even began to contemplate a replacement. But, even a month after Charles had abandoned me—us—I was not yet ready to look for a surrogate cat.

Instead, I went into what could be called my default mode: reason. I would analyze such matters as the nature of cats and the history of my relationship with Charles. I began with some soul-searching, possibly a vestige of the guilt phase.

"Hmm," I thought, making the archetypal gesture of scratching my bearded chin. "Maybe, I enabled Charles' sneaky, tricky side." I readily identified two cat archetypes in my own psyche: Felix and Simone Signoret. As a child, I had counted Felix among my favorite tricksters, along with Bugs Bunny and Charlie Chaplin. As for Simone Signoret, she possibly represented a far more complex model for my relationship with Charles.

From *Cat People*, a beloved horror movie, I recalled her as a sexy seducer who, once you were seduced, turned into a black panther and jealously attacked both you and any rival for your affections. The wonderful scene of menace in the indoor swimming pool (filmed, as it happens, five blocks from my own brownstone, in Manhattan) still had great resonance for me, perhaps because, over the years, I had watched the movie several times.

My feelings about this resonance are, I confess, extremely vague, but I think I may identify the pool with my garden, and the rival fleeing the pool with my pets scampering off. What I clearly remember from the scene is that a kitten morphs into a panther, which in turn becomes the Simone Signoret character. It is left unclear whether it is panther or woman who rends the bathrobe of a rival. As the blonde attendant comments to the victim, "Gee, whiz, Honey, it's torn to ribbons." Finally, is it worth mentioning that this movie originally came out in 1942, the year of my birth, and that the birth was attended by jealousy on the part of my paranoid father, who thought I looked like the obstetrician?

Jealousy—was that it? One afternoon, without bothering to don my raincoat or dark glasses, I rushed to a local bookstore, where I bought an armful of those odious, neo-*Reader's Digest* magazines about pets. Back in my chair, I read that cat owners who introduce a "companion" into their cat's habitat often inadvertently trigger stress in the first cat, sometimes taking the form of skin irritations and bladder infections. Since Charles had already been my pet kitten when I introduced puppy Muffin into the apartment, could the disappearance of the former have been caused by long-simmering resentment of the latter? But how could I even begin to determine if this were true? (Asking Charles to lie down on the couch would be quixotic, not to mention redundant.)

After reading several more articles about feline jealousy and somatization, I was still in the realm of vague speculation. What my reading did reveal was that very little is known about the cat-human nexus. What *is* known is that people and dogs have much more fully developed relationships. So, whimsical as ever, I decided to consult Muffin. What harm could it do? Snapping my fingers, I summoned him from his bed.

Stroking him once or twice, I asked, "Muffin, was Charles jealous of you?" The dog's brow furrowed, and he whimpered. But, of course, since he did not nod his head in the affirmative, or shake it in the negative (both of which he had done in the past), I was really no closer to an answer. If anything, the whimpering might have meant that he still remembered, and missed, Charles. Or, to stretch a point, it might have been an expression of empathy with my own loss.

I hit the magazines again. Amidst all the sentimentality and half-baked speculation, I arrived at two more solid facts: cats are undeniably playful, and they will only run away if sorely mistreated. Putting these facts together, I drew an inference: Charles might have jumped out through the garden door that night to play a joke on me, but he would not have stayed away, at least not of his own volition. That led right back to the pair of sad possibilities I had considered at the outset: either he was dead, or he had been kidnapped. (I won't say cat-napped.)

Questions always seem to lead to more questions: whose idea had it been to run out into the garden in the first place? To that, my answer was, perhaps surprisingly, Muffin. Dogs are more sensitive to their owners' thoughts and feelings. Muffin might even have heard—in the ill-fated story I wrote and read to them—a fugitive wish on my part to *make* my pets run away.

But why would I have wished for that? Well, to be honest, like any relationship, this one had its negatives. I enjoy travel, but owning two pets and having no close friends whom I could ask to care for them, my traveling had been limited to a maximum of two nights at a time. On these occasions, I would leave food and water for Charles, but Muffin required an expensive kennel stay, from which he always returned needy and sad.

Why the kennel? The first time I had gone off for a weekend, to a distant cousin's funeral in (yes) Charleston, I had left food and water for them both. Perhaps, it was because I had not known much about puppy and kitten training, but I had, in no way, prepared my animals for this separation. When I got home, the place was a mess. Charles had used his box, eaten most of his food, and drunk most of his water. But Muffin had shat on the floor next to his box—a statement—and had tipped over both his food and water bowls, creating another smeary mess on the kitchen floor (luckily, tile).

Thus, my hypothesis that, if either of them had instigated the garden scamper, it must have been the dog. Of course, it was a short step to explaining what happened next. Muffin's loyalty brought him right back inside, whereas Charles' playful independence precipitated his leap to freedom.

Asking, again, why my well-treated cat had not returned to his food source by now, and combining that question with all of my newfound ideas, I was led to a plan of action: I would methodically question the neighbors to find out who had kidnapped, and possibly murdered, Charles.

* * *

THERE WERE THREE other apartments in my building, which I owned: rentals on the second, third, and top floors. Emulating the literary detectives I admire most (Lord Peter Wimsey and Philip Marlowe), I would begin with the most likely suspect. Once before, Charles had escaped and tipped over a milk bottle, breaking it and spilling the contents onto the mat in front of the door of the second-floor apartment. The tenant was a choleric old woman whose only child, a grown son, lived in Florida and (in her words), "Never visits, never calls, never so much as sends his mother a goddamn email."

At nine-thirty on a Wednesday morning, thirty-three days after Charles' disappearance, I climbed the stairs to the second floor and rang the bell.

## Part Three

AS I HEARD feet shuffling toward me, I thought again about the minds of cats. Envy, yes; shame, no. Disappointment, yes; regret, no. My lucubrations were cut short by my neighbor's arrival at the door. "Who?" she called. I told her, then waited while she undid three or four locks and opened the door a crack. She was wearing fuzzy pink slippers and a matching bathrobe, and her white hair was rolled in orange curlers. Girding myself to launch into the speech I had prepared, I hesitated, intimidated by her scowling silence. Since her rent checks had always been mailed to me promptly, and since I, in turn, kept the building in tip-top shape, instructing my handyman to perform assiduous routine maintenance in order to pre-empt the need for costly repairs, my interactions with this neighbor, when we happened to meet in the vestibule or in front of the building, were limited to token exchanges (like the grumbling about her son).

Now the atmosphere was blatantly adversarial. I ventured a smile that I hoped would be reassuring, but, if anything, her scowl deepened. Then, I heard it, a blood-chilling yowl from somewhere in the rear of the apartment.

If this were one of those who-done-its I have mentioned, the yowl, unmistakably issuing from the throat of my beloved Charles, would have turned out to be either the first in a chain of red herrings, or the solution of the mystery, to which, after a series of tortuous and amusing detours, the writer would return at the end of the story. But this was real life.

When I heard that horrible noise, a conditioned reflex kicked in. Charles' yowls, I knew, were normally attempts to manipulate me. For example, he would yowl if the second half of a can of food was not fresh enough for him, or if I did not scratch the precise millimeter under his chin that gave him maximum pleasure. This time, the manipulation must be a cry for help. Having heard my voice when I addressed the tenant, Charles was crying out for me to rescue him.

"My, my, Mrs —," I began, trying to be cagey. "I never knew *you* had a cat."

"Well, Sonny," she replied. (I was not more than a few years younger than she.) "I guess you live and you learn." And she slammed the door in my face. But I was not so easily put off.

Pressing my ear to the door, I could tell from her stertorous breathing that she was still on the other side. In my firmest, most no-nonsense voice, I borrowed from the hostage situations about which I had read in *policiers*. "Are you listening, Mrs.—?" No reply. "I know you have my cat in there." Still nothing. "If you'll just hand him out, you may still be able to avoid some extremely unpleasant consequences." Did her breathing grow louder? "What I mean is, I will summon the police. And, as you know, since I am your landlord, I have the legal right to demand access to your apartment in an emergency, which I consider the theft of my cat to be." A sigh. Was she weakening? "In that event, I will not only immediately institute eviction proceedings, but I will press criminal charges that could result in your conviction for a felony offense, punishable by up to ten-to-twelve years in prison. Do you understand me, Madam?"

This farrago of legalese gobbledygook finally had an effect. "Well," she said in a furious voice, "you can just go fuck yourself." Then, I heard her padding rapidly away down the hall inside the apartment. A few seconds later, I heard a series of yowls, which suddenly grew louder, presumably because she had opened the door to the room in which Charles was being held captive.

What should I do? I had a horrible premonition that my tenant was about to have a panic attack and murder my cat. Luckily, I had had the foresight to bring my passkeys with me, and fumbling at one of the two exterior locks, in a few seconds I had it open. But I realized that I did not have a key for the other lock, which she must have had installed without my permission.

Then, I heard another expletive and, I could have sworn, the sound of scrabbling claws racing toward me. This time, instead of yowls, there were a series of loud meows that sounded increasingly desperate, followed by the sound of the slippered feet, running now.

"All right, all right," she said. "Hold your horses, I'm coming." Fumbling with the locks, she cursed again when the door did not open.

"The top one is already unlocked," I said, assuming she must have re-locked it. A second later, I heard another click, and pushing the door open, I was met by Charles, who flew into my arms. The poor cat smelled like fetid dust and looked awful. He was thin and filthy, and his white blaze and paws were soot colored. His expression mixed extreme consternation with what can only be called profound relief and gratitude. My neighbor witnessed this touching reunion with a mixed expression of her own, scorn and fear.

"I'll deal with you later," I said, and leaving her at the door, I cradled Charles in my arms and carried him downstairs.

* * *

THE AFTERMATH AND explanation can be narrated readily. After Charles had wolfed down three-quarters of a can of his favorite food—kidney-and-bacon (wet)—he spent half an hour restoring his coat to pristineness. Meanwhile, Muffin keened with excitement. I could see him struggling to contain his ardent happiness as he observed the return and revival of his best friend. With his usual sensitivity, he did not yet try to engage Charles in play. Touchingly, their first interaction occurred while Charles was still busy washing himself. The big dog lay down beside him and gave the cat's face a loving flick of his big pink tongue. Totally out of character, the cat tolerated this invasion of his personal space.

When Charles was completely clean, he clicked off to the kitchen, and to his box, which I had left in its usual place. Urinating only (he would presumably proceed to his other business when the trauma lifted), he rejoined us in the living room, where he stretched, yawned, hopped onto the couch, and closed his eyes. Stationing himself on the rug, and snuggling up to the cat's resting place, Muffin assumed the role of sentinel. As for me, settling down in my armchair, I just watched. Once again, all was right with the world.

Over the next several days, I thought about my neighbor, whom I did not see. Gradually, my vengeful impulses were replaced by empathy. I thought I understood her loneliness all too well. I wound up knocking on her door again, this time to invite her down for a cup of tea, explaining first that I had decided to let bygones be bygones. Her expression of relief was lovely to behold. Worried, however, that she might be deranged,

I knew that I must initiate an exploratory conversation to determine whether my pets and I would be safe if I allowed her to remain in the building.

* * *

"HAVE ANOTHER PIECE of pound cake, Mrs. —," I encouraged her. Charles was hidden behind the skirts of the sofa, in front of which Muffin once again stood guard. The woman was seated in a small Windsor chair that matched my own, larger chair. "It's good, I hope?" I had baked it myself. With an affirmative nod, she accepted a second piece, took a small bite, and washed it down with a gulp of tea. Instead of the dressing gown and curlers, today she was wearing an old-fashioned navy-blue suit and matching pillbox hat. The hat, especially, which must have been at least three decades old, looked very chic. Not just her appearance, but her demeanor and behavior during this visit were revelations to me. People, like pets, can be full of surprises.

After giving her time to swallow, and speaking very softly, I posed the question I had been waiting to ask. "Why did you take my cat, Mrs. —?"

She blushed crimson, avoiding eye contact. Charles stayed where he was, and Muffin eyed the visitor warily. Carefully placing cup and saucer on the coffee table between us, she replied, speaking as softly as I had. "I'm very sorry for that, Mr. —. All I can say is that one day, about a month ago, I returned home to find the cat just outside the building. I was surprised to see him there."

So far, she sounded completely sane. "When I opened the front door, he followed me in, and then stopped at your door. I rang your bell and, when you did not answer, I assumed you were out." She paused for a deep sigh. "I'm not sure why I did what I did next. I went upstairs and found some leftover chicken in my fridge. Cutting it into small pieces and putting it on a plastic

85

plate, I opened the door and called to the cat. Since I did not yet know his name, I just said, 'Pss, pss, pss.' And he came bounding right up the stairs." Another sigh accompanied by a furtive glance to see how I was taking all this. "I had placed the food just inside my door, and very slowly, with great caution, he stepped into the apartment." Again, she paused, this time looking sad.

"Well," I said encouragingly, "That was very kind of you, Mrs. —. But why…"

"It was very *wrong* of me," she burst out. "Very. At first, I just thought I'd let the cat stay in the apartment until you got home, and then return him. But…you were out for such a long time that day."

It occurred to me that this must have been the day I had had the notices printed, and then gone around the neighborhood posting them. I remembered that I had not returned until well after dark.

"And then, the next day, I saw your notices about…Charles…everywhere, and realized what must have happened. After that…" She began to sob. I gestured to the box of Kleenex I had placed on the coffee table, and, taking a handful, she dried her eyes. "Thank you," she said. "You're very kind." Gathering herself, she continued. "After that, every day I would tell myself I should return the cat to his rightful owner. I mean, he looked so unhappy. I could hardly get him to eat or to clean himself. But…but…but…he's such a wonderful animal, Mr. —. And I was so lonely. I don't know how to…I'm so sorry." And she began to sob again.

"There, there, Mrs.—.," I said, reaching across to pat her hand. At that point, Charles's triangular face emerged from beneath the sofa. Muffin remained on guard. "I completely understand. Please don't worry. As far as I'm concerned, the incident is over."

"You're a sweet man," she said (which was true), and we resumed our tea party. The next day, I accompanied Mrs. — to a nearby animal shelter, where I helped her select a kitten.

## Epilogue

SEVERAL MORE WEEKS have now passed, during which I have assumed the role of mentor, training Mrs. — in the finer points of animal care. Tomorrow will be a very special day. I have invited my new friend down for brunch, instructing her to bring along her kitten, whose name is Timmy, for a play date. I plan to spend the interim preparing treats for everyone, and trying to think of ways to make the introduction of this stranger-kitten into the home of Charles and Muffin as harmonious as possible.

By evening, having baked again (an upside-down peach cake), and having returned from shopping for the animals, I found myself becoming trepidatious about Timmy's visit. So, dipping into the wicker rack, I dug out a handful of the pet magazines, and once again settled into my chair. Muffin and Charles were similarly ensconced in their regular places.

Inspiration struck. Recalling some of the facts I had read in one of those odious articles, I would now reread them—aloud— to those whom they would touch most closely. First, I made sure that both the front door of the apartment and the one leading to the garden were firmly secured. Then, I began to read:

"Among the most common sources of stress in pets is the misguided attempt to introduce a new animal into their midst. This often stems from a well-meaning attempt to enrich the social lives…"

Looking up to gauge whether my recital was having any effect, I saw the tip of Charles' tail as he scampered under the sofa. And as I watched, Muffin ostentatiously rolled his heavy body over in his bed, so that his back was facing me. The next lines in the article stuck in my throat:

"Cats may experience disappointment, but not regret. The single exception is that they most likely regret not being large enough to eat us."

## The End

# III. ACTIVISM

"…if vicious people are united and constitute a power, then honest folk must do the same. That's simple enough."
–Leo Tolstoy[18]

IN OTHER WORDS, progressive causes call for unified, concerted action. Activism also serves the Gravy-ite project of getting a life. Given our reading, our thoughtfulness, abundant free time, desire to remain relevant, and who-knows-what-else, many of us are fringe players, at least, in the game of politics. We give money to "good causes," we sign petitions, write letters, add our (weak) voices at demonstrations, and walk (as far as we can) on marches. "Disposable income" is, perhaps, another key ingredient in this enthusiasm for public affairs. However, by no means does the moneyed class of Gravy-ites exclusively consist of political progressives. Far from it.

## The Tigers of Yerevan

GIVEN THE CONDITIONS under which he labors, it is no wonder that the performance of Señor Hector Babineau, Manager of the Hillendale Hobby Club (HHC), tends toward the erratic. Not only is he slave to the whims of forty-some supervisors, but the salary attached to his position is pathetic. Ardent hobbyists all, the Club members also act as if their own amateurism should prompt our guest speakers to appear free of

---

[18] *War and Peace*, Simon & Schuster, NY, 1942, transl. Aylmer Maude, p.1308

charge. Like most people who love money, they seem unable to understand why anyone else might want some. Even the rent we pay to the Congregational Church, where we hold our bi-monthly meetings, is a pittance.

As for me, I am so rich that I have long since overcome the prejudices of my class. The juggling chimp, the blind hypnotist, the born-again erstwhile serial murderer, the savant who can multiply seven-digit numbers in his head—they all have to eat. As Vice-President, I have proposed to the Board that, in order to beef up Señor Babineau's salary, each member be assessed a hundred dollars, which is chump change to the residents of our exclusive enclave. But, no. Pennywise...

* * *

ON AT LEAST one recent occasion, Babineau may have come a cropper—or, on second thought, he may have scored a coup.

"It is my pleasure to introduce to you this evening, ladies and gentlemen of the Hillendale Hobby Club, the eminent graphologist, Gospodin Imra Dikovitch. Mr. Dikovitch is President of ..."

As he rambled on in his high, whinnying voice, instead of listening to Señor Babineau, I scrutinized him and the guest. Since they were standing side by side directly in front of us, and since, as usual, I was seated front-row center, I had an excellent vantage point. They were about the same age and height—fiftyish and short. The portly Babineau wore his dyed and Brilliantined black hair shoulder length. That night, he was clad in a shiny teal suit with a fat pink tie, navy shirt, and mock-alligator loafers. Skinny Mr. Dikovitch was also a "dude," but a dude of a different stripe, sporting a goatee and black polo shirt, black tuxedo top, tight black jeans, and tooled cordovan cowboy boots.

When he finally began to speak, it was in a muttered bass with faintly central or eastern European inflections. Unlike Babineau, Dikovitch cut directly to the chase. Meanwhile, the manager tiptoed up the central aisle of the church to where an old-fashioned slide projector sat on a small wooden table.

"I am here tonight, good people, to present a graphological analysis of the writings of the esteemed Armenian novelist, Arakel Arslanian, who lived from 1861 to 1957. With the recent resurgence of Arslanian's reputation in eastern Europe, and with the imminent publication in U.K. of his most popular novel, which will appear under the title, *The Tigers of Yerevan*, it seems more important than ever for readers to understand the great man's psyche. In a way, to do so is a form of *caveat lector*. Why do I say this? Because, not to put too fine a point, *Paron*—Mister—Arslanian was a homicidal maniac." I could almost hear the members' ears twitching. "First slide, please."

The lights were lowered, and, turning in my seat, I could see Babineau's round face, illuminated by the bulb on the projector. A few seconds later, a manuscript page in a language unfamiliar to me appeared on the fold-up screen beside the speaker. The first characters were these:

Ա Ի Լ  Խ  Ծ  Կ  Հ  Ձ  Ղ  Ճ  Մ  Յ  Ն  Ծ
Ո  Չ  Պ  Ջ  Ռ  Ս  Վ  Տ.

(Lest you think I am a polyglot genius, I should explain that I photographed the slide with my phone.)

Using a wooden pointer, Dikovitch began. "Take the fifth character, "Ծ," which is the equivalent in Hayeren, the Armenian language, of 'E' in the Latin alphabet. You will note the violent sweep of the first, downward stroke. Is it any coincidence that this is the initial letter of 'mayr,' the Hayeren word for 'mother?'

May I inform you that Arslanian's mother was rumored for many years before her death of being a practitioner of human sacrifice, a witch?" He paused melodramatically.

"Next, let us consider a second word: սպանություն. This time all the letters, including the initial ones, are formed in a soft, looping handwriting, which evokes the feeling of the calligraphy of classical Arabic love poetry. սպանություն is the Hayeren word for 'murder.'"

Dikovitch nattered on in this vein for another eight or ten minutes. Then, he abruptly stopped. "Lights," he commanded. Turning the projector off, and the lights back on, Señor Babineau came trotting toward the front, clapping his hands loudly.

"Please, everyone," he said, "put your hands together for our wonderful guest, Professor Imra Dikovitch."

While the manager heartily pumped the speaker's hand, the audience applauded with an enthusiasm normally reserved for sympathetic politicians. Babineau called for comments and questions. Several hands shot up, and he pointed to a bejeweled, matronly woman in the second row, a few seats to my right. I recognized her from the nearby country club, the HCC, where, on several occasions, I had seen her hitting golf balls into a practice net.

"That was fascinating, Professor," she said with a smile. Her bracelets jangled, and Dikovitch made a courtly little bow. "But tell us, please, how your analysis might affect our reading of Mr. Arsenal's—"

"Arslanian," Dikovitch corrected.

"…of Mr. Arsalan's novel?"

"Excellent question," exclaimed Babineau, peering at the guest with exaggerated interest. To me, the question was obvious. Dikovitch's answer was not.

"Well, madam," he said, "assuming that you really intend to read *The Tigers of Yerevan,* I suggest that you approach this book with extreme caution. The main plot is a retelling of the Romeo and Juliet story, in this case depicting love between representatives of nationalities who are mortal enemies, an Armenian and an Azeri. Well, it would be easy to infer that this story is a plea for peace and harmony. Doesn't that sound nice? But such an inference would be a gross misreading. Properly understood, *The Tigers of Yerevan* subtly invites the reader to draw from the poisonous history of enmity which leads to the death of the lovers, the lesson that both sides are completely justified in slaughtering each other and should continue to do so, full speed ahead. *Tigers of Yerevan* is by no means what you would call 'progressive' novel."

After several, less consequential questions, the evening ended with a second round of applause. Consulting his watch, *Gospodin* Dikovitch accepted an envelope from the manager and departed. Babineau rushed over to the refreshment table and began to stuff his face. On important items, such as food and drink, the Club does not stint. I joined him at the table.

"Well, Peter," he crowed. "So how was that one? Not bad, eh?"

"Very interesting." I swallowed half of a delicious pig-in-a-blanket and washed it down with a swig of white wine. "But how do we know whether to believe this 'expert?' After all, he may have his own fish to fry."

That brought Babineau up short. Raising his eyebrows, he swallowed what was in his mouth before replying. "He came with excellent references, including one from a personal friend of mine in Columbia University's Department of Linguistics."

"Well, 'excellent references' could be beside the point. They may suggest that he knows his stuff, but not that what he told us was true. I have a suggestion."

"Shoot," said Babineau, crunching a carrot.

"For one of our upcoming sessions, why not invite a medium? Perhaps, such a person would be able to channel Arslanian's spirit. Maybe, she—I assume—could even ask him about his mother. At least, she could bring up the supposed subtext of *The Tigers of Yerevan*." I confess that I was being half-facetious. My serious half really wanted to learn more. Both halves, as usual, wanted to be amused.

"Hmm," said Babineau. "Interesting idea. Let me look into it, Peter, and get back to you." Putting his smile in place, with quick little footsteps, he hurried off in the direction of the Helen whose question had launched these ships. I went home.

* * *

TWO WEEKS LATER, the phone rang. It was about nine and, having finished supper, I was in my study reading C.V. Wedgwood's excellent history of the Thirty Years' War.

"Mr. Vice-President," a familiar voice announced, "this is your servant, Babineau." Sometimes, you could not tell whether the manager was being unctuous or ironic. "I have found the very person you suggested."

"Oh?" Not that I had forgotten, but I was still surprised.

"Yes, the medium. Even better, an *Armenian* medium. I found her in a storefront on East 56th Street, in Manhattan. I was on my way to meet some friends for dinner. Her name is Anoush Baklavarian. 'Anoush' means 'sweet' in Hayeren, by the way."

"You don't say. Have you signed her up?"

"Well, not yet. You see, her fee is a bit…steep. As per Ms. Sheridan's instructions, I am currently engaged in delicate negotiations with Ms. Baklavarian." Colleen Sheridan is President of the HHC.

"Look, just sign her up, I'll pay the difference. I'm really interested in what she might have to say."

I could almost hear Señor Babineau bursting into a radiant smile. "Yes, certainly," he said. "It will be a matter of one-hundred dollars above the usual fee."

"You mean, twenty-five for the medium and seventy-five for you?" I was only half joking.

"Mr. Peter, please. I am a man of probity. Do you think I would have taken the position of Manager of the HHC if I were a mercenary kind of person? If not for my day job, I would be starving."

"Don't make me cry, Señor Babineau. Anyway, sign her up."

* * *

TWO MONTHS LATER, and one minute late, the assembled members buzzed with anticipation. Any moment now, Señor Babineau would make his typically flamboyant entrance through the swinging double doors leading in from the church vestibule. I was in my usual place. Like most of the other members (except the infirm), I was standing and peering back toward the doors. What came through them was like a wedding procession—a very peculiar one.

Tonight, Babineau wore a special outfit that I had not seen before. It combined a baggy white suit with a rakish Panama hat. At his side waddled a fat old woman wearing a special outfit of her own. The main garment was a voluminous black, white, red, and yellow gown with something like pleats in the front. From beneath her buff-colored shawl peeped a pair of silver earrings, set with what looked to be ping-pong ball sized pearls. Although she leaned on a silver-tipped wooden cane, Babineau was supporting the woman, presumably Ms. Anoush Baklavarian, by the elbow. There was a murmur from the membership when we realized she was blind.

One of the round white plastic card tables normally stored in the basement had been set up in front, surrounded by eight folding chairs. Babineau led Ms. Baklavarian around the table, and, tapping with her cane, she subsided into the chair directly facing the audience—us. After an anomalously succinct introduction, the manager asked for six volunteers. He then sat down on the chair to the medium's right.

About twenty members, myself included, rushed to the front. We soon sorted ourselves out, however: six of us took the remaining chairs at the table. The sorting principle appeared to be a combination of age and wealth. At least, none of the six was under sixty or a non-multi-millionaire. As soon as we were seated, Babineau clapped his hands, and someone in back dimmed the lights. Without further ceremony, in a resonant, heavily accented contralto, Mme. Baklavarian launched the proceedings. (I cannot keep referring to this guest as "Ms." Politically correct though the appellation may be, in this case, it is just too incongruous.)

"Mr. Babinetti has already explained why you invited me to come here this evening." Although he flinched, Babineau did not correct her. I thought the mistake might have been intentional, some kind of joke. "Everyone at the table will please join hands." The medium closed her eyes and grasped Babineau's hand and that of the woman to her left, the bejeweled golfer. I could sense among the six of us a certain reluctance to take our neighbors' hands, a reluctance I confess I shared. After all, ours is the land of power handshakes and air kisses. But Mme. Baklavarian brooked no hesitation.

"Please, everyone," she ordered, "do as you are told. If you are unwilling to accept my authority, what you have asked me to do will be impossible, and I will leave immediately." Although it did not matter to me, I was sure she would not forego the fee.

But it didn't come to that. We all quickly, if squeamishly, joined hands.

"Are we ready, then?" she asked.

"Ready," Babineau replied.

Without further ado, Mme. Baklavarian launched into what I recognized from countless books and movies as a garden-variety séance. I will spare the reader the hackneyed details: the mumbled entreaties, disclaimers when nothing happened, and renewed entreaties. Finally, there was a rattling of the table, as either Mme. Baklavarian set off a chain reaction by violently shaking her neighbors' hands—or the invisible ghost of the writer, Arakel Arslanian, rumbled into our midst. Aside from this rattling, there was not the slightest sound from either the occupants of the table or the spectators.

Mme. Baklavarian began the séance proper by addressing a few reassuring-sounding words to our guest. Although she spoke (presumably) in Hayeren, she provided us with a running translation. "I have apologized to Paron—to Mister— Arslanian for disturbing his rest this evening and asked him whether he might be willing to answer a few questions."

Having said that much, and with our hands still shaking, she cocked her ear toward something just above—as it happened— my right shoulder. I felt a sort of shudder behind me (or was it my own shudder?), and, after a few seconds, she translated the specter's putative response.

"He says he is not certain he will be able to oblige us. He feels hostility at the table, and wonders whether we can suspend our disbelief." She cocked her ear again, spoke into the air, waited, then translated. The shuddering continued. "In fact, if not for my own kind entreaties, he says, he would already have fled back to his own realm." Again, the ear was cocked; again, she translated. "Only because he has something very important to impart has he given us this second chance." Starting on her left, the medium appeared slowly to scan the table with her sightless eyes. Stopping when she reached the bejeweled matron, she asked, "Well?"

The matron, who looked as if she were trying to keep under control an excitement that could almost have been sexual, whispered her reply. "I am now prepared to believe our visitor."

Mme. Baklavarian's blind gaze continued slowly around the table. I confess to a certain *frisson* of my own, but, by the time she reached my place, which was the last one before Babineau's, and stopped again, I had composed myself. Without waiting for her to ask, I said, in what I hoped was a calm voice, "I am also ready, Madame. I apologize to our esteemed guest."

Once again, she addressed the ghost, this time at some length. Then, she said to us, "I have made your apologies, and I have reiterated exactly what we hope he will tell us."

By now, the shaking at the table had subsided. The medium cocked her ear toward the empty space above us, and, for several minutes, appeared to listen intently. Then, she spoke briefly, apparently asking another question, and listened to Arslanian's long reply. Finally, she brought her blind gaze back down to our level.

"He has now responded. He begs us to release him from the ordeal that his return to the realm of the living has inflicted upon him. But, since what he has told me is so important, he suggests that, if there are further questions, we should give him a few years to recover, after which we can try to summon his spirit again."

That, somehow, seemed funny, maybe because it occurred to me that, in a few years, several of the older members, myself included, might have joined the great Armenian novelist on the other side, which would obviate the need for a second séance. I was not alone: there were titters from the audience. Once again, our hands began to tremble, this time even more violently. Mme. Baklavarian shook her head in obvious disgust, dropped her neighbors' hands, and muttered what I can only assume was a Hayeren imprecation.

"That did it," she announced. "Paron Arslanian has departed in a—how do you call it?—chuff."

"But what did he say before he left?" two of us simultaneously asked. The assembled membership murmured its assent.

"Yes, of course, I will tell you this," she replied. "And I think you will be impressed." There was absolute silence; the medium had us eating from her hand. "As requested, I asked Paron Arslanian to speak about his work, specifically his masterpiece, *The Tigers of Yerevan*. Although I am unable to quote his exact reply, I will give you the jest of it." No one so much as coughed.

"He did not deny that the underlying message of his novel is that the Armenians and Azeris are both culpable for the Nagorno-Karabakh War. He believes, without regret, that the conflict will end only when the two sides have destroyed one another. He went on to generalize from this war, to speak of the Israelis and Palestinians, Indians and Pakistanis, Irish and English, and so forth. His message was the same for each conflict: a curse on both sides, a wish to see them obliterated from the Earth in an orgy of mutual destruction."

For several seconds, the room was silent. Then came what was, perhaps, the biggest surprise of all. "But Paron Arslanian ended his diatribe with a—how do you say—a beatnik-ific, no, beautif…"

"Beatific," I prompted.

"Thank you. I cannot remember all of his examples, but he be-a-ti-fi-cal-ly imagined the Earth without any human beings. Do you remember the Bible passage where the Lord…" (she hastily crossed herself) "… throws back the curtain and reveals the glory of creation to his faithful servant, Job? Well, it was like that.

"Paron Arslanian described many creatures: a rhinoceros peering nearsightedly through the tall grass of a savannah, a crane standing like a sentinel on one thin leg in a lovely marsh, swallows darting across the sky at dusk, elephants on the bank of a river splashing each other playfully…and many other such pictures. He was in the midst of describing a giraffe bending gracefully toward the tender leaves of a small tree when he became exhausted. Then, you laughed and drove him away."

With her blind eyes, Mme. Baklavarian looked out at the crowd reproachfully. Without another word, leaning heavily on her cane, she rose. Señor Babineau scrambled to his feet. Again, he took her by the elbow, and, to somewhat ambivalent applause, the tandem toddled back toward the double doors. We all remained silent; the only sound was the tapping of the seer's cane. The expression on most of our faces is perhaps best expressed by that famous phrase from Keats: "a look of wild surmise."

After a few moments, President Sheridan stood up and, muttering a few words about "our most interesting guest," she announced the date of the next meeting—"speaker TBA"—and sent us all on our way. Exiting the church as quickly as the slow crush permitted, I saw no sign of Señor Babineau or Mme. Baklavarian. I assumed he was guiding her to the train station, which is about a hundred yards from the church. It was a pleasant evening, cool for mid-summer, so I strolled back toward my house, which is in the opposite direction from the station, and less than a mile from the church.

* * *

TWO MONTHS HAVE passed. Apocalyptic though the diatribe of the ghost of Arakel Arslanian may have been, it was, in a sense, even-handed. The Armenian certainly seemed free of any obvious political bias, unless you could call him a rhinoceros-ophile, or something. Of course, we have only the word of the medium, Mme. Baklavarian, for all this. But I must say that I, usually skeptical to the bone, did sense a certain…force around the table that evening.

## The End

OF COURSE, IN the current political climate, those of us who *are* progressives risk inciting the fury of our leader, whose fury needs no incitement, and whose happiness, such as it is, seems to depend on the unhappiness of others. Consider this fantasy-scenario:

**The Real Enemy Within:**

**INTERNAL MEMO**
**HIGHLY CONFIDENTIAL**
**(LEAK, AND YOU'RE TOAST)**

**New York, New York, August 24<sup>th</sup>, 2018**

**From: RS, Long-Term Planning Director**

**To: Office of the President**

**Subject: Another New Initiative**

Good morning, Mr. P! The birds are tweeting, and so are we. Here's another really big idea.

Now that the Wall is finally up, and we're having difficulties replacing stoop laborers (*los piscadores*), why not set our sights on a group that is leeching away far more jobs than lettuce and strawberry pickers? And this time, I'm talking jobs any real American would love.

I refer to our senior citizens, whose unpaid work in many sectors is snatching the bread from the mouths of the unemployed. The fact that seniors can do these jobs shows how easy they are. Examples: answering phones, checking library books in and out, museum guides, tutoring youth (not *immigrant* youth, anymore), voter registration and poll watching (heh, heh), handing out Bingo cards, etc. etc.

My suggestion is simple. Let's deport this parasitic section of the population. Not just for the jobs. As the fake press keeps crowing, many of these folks dominate the so-called "protest" marches—directed at *you,* sir.

Where should we send them? Since we all have parents of our own, many still living, we can't just use deserts, radioactive islands, or Antarctica. May I propose, instead, the AARP (Assorted Anterior Russian Pissholes), i.e., the former Soviet "stans," which many of these fogeys came from in the first place?

The plan would have humongous side benefits.

1. Financial: getting rid of millions of Medicare freeloaders would instantly close the you-know-what gap. Even if we ponied up to subsidize the salaries of the non-age impaired replacement workers, the cost would be a drop in the budgetary bucket—much less than those foreign aid grants you recently put the kibosh on.

2. Political: keeping the "temples of culture" open would placate the urban elite.

Of course, there's one obvious snag: unlike the illegals we're getting rid of, *these folks vote.* (45% of the electorate, in 2016.) Not to worry. Combining the tests required in some states for drivers' license renewal with citizenship tests (which we know and love), we could institute senior voting qualification tests that would disqualify millions of the old farts. Sample questions: *Not,* Who was the eleventh President? What does the first amendment guarantee? (I can't answer either of those, myself.) *But,* what is your name? (Wrong. You skipped the middle initial.) What did you have for breakfast? (Wrong: *Medium-*boiled eggs.)

It might be tricky, but I bet we could key the plan to family values: "Now your senior loved ones can escape the contentious climate of our beleaguered nation." (Get Steve back on board for this kind of spin.)

In conclusion: Say the word, sir, and I'll set things in motion. And, if this memo is TMI, I can shoot you a 50-word summary. (BTW, I certainly don't think of *you* as a Golden Ager, Mr. P.)

As always,
Yr Mst Fthfl Srvnt,
RS (LTPD)

**The End**

EVEN IF MASS deportation is not really in the cards, our culture finds subtler ways to maroon Gravy-ites on The Desert Isle of Age. Activism serves as a strong counterforce, a means of connecting with the like-minded, creating self-selected communities that resemble families both in their love and in their bickering. Such groups may also be forums in which to indulge our bibliophilia:

## A Little Learning (or Knowledge)

"A little learning is a dangerous thing,
Drink deep, or taste not the Pierian spring."[19]

## January 2017:

"'A LITTLE LEARNING,'" (pompous) Jerry intones, "'is a dangerous thing. Drink deep or taste not the…something or other…spring.'"

"'Pī-ˈir-ē-ən,'" I (the pedant) contribute.

"Cor-rect," says (factual) Joan, googling the name on her phone. "'A spring sacred to the Muses, the source of knowledge and the arts.'"

Evan (our young wag) chimes in: "That quotation is so righteous."

"Yes, but it's usually *mis*quoted," (wry) Charlotte observes. "Most people say, 'a little knowledge.' Maybe, they should drink deeper." At least, she does not add, "Bill should have."

Like the Dirty Dozen in the WW2 movie, each of us has our own specialty.

---

[19] Alexander Pope, *Essay on Criticism* (London: W. Lewis, 1711), ll.218-19

* * *

THE "SPRING" FOR this repartee was a small mistake we—I—had detected at the October meeting of our book club, about a month before the elections. Our venue is always the same, because only Joan's living room can accommodate us all, what with our texts, note-taking devices (iPads, paper pads), back pillows, etc.—plus refreshments, which we take turns providing. On the evening in question, Jerry had brought *biscotti.* Joan, as usual, had served the coffee (decaf).

We also rotate the task of opening discussion with a summary of the book, despite the presumption that we have all read it. In October, there were two books: *A Short History of Sicily* by Timothy Bottomsley,[20] an Englishman who had lived on the island for several decades; and *A Concise History of Vietnam* by Angela Rothstein,[21] a Professor at I-Forget-the-Name College. One reason for doubling up was that both books were, well, short: 170 pages (Sicily), and 183 (Vietnam). Another was that two of our members, Jerry and Charlotte, were about to visit, respectively, the places in question.

Doubling up was what caused Bill's mistake, which did not really have much to do with "a little learning." Describing a period in the late Seventeenth Century in one of the three provinces that would eventually coalesce into Vietnam, he said that, after a tumultuous interlude, social and political issues were placed on hold, while the government of the day wrestled with problems of food and taxation. But his notes must have been

---

[20] Original source material: Peter Sammartino and William Roberts, *Sicily, An Informal History* (Cornwall Books, New York, 1992).

[21] Original source material: Christopher Goscha, *Vietnam, A New History* (Basic Books, New York, 2016)

garbled: that passage actually refers to the period leading up to the Messina Revolt, in Sicily.

Bill's mistake was also explained by the fact that the histories of both places feature very few periods that can*not* be called "tumultuous interludes." But, in addition to famine and high taxes, the passage in Rothstein mentions corruption, and that ubiquitous factor in Sicilian history appears to have been missing, for once—according to Bottomsley—in the lead-up to the Messina Revolt.

The similarity between Sicilian and Vietnamese history made Bill's task the most complicated in the six-month history of the club. True, *O'Oh*, the post-modern Irish novel we discussed a few weeks ago, is pretty opaque, but that was later, and Charlotte, who drew the short straw, is not only adept at fudging, but after Bill's gaffe, she was particularly careful. Anyway…

✳ ✳ ✳

THE AFTERMATH OF the November elections in our own country has also been, to put it mildly, tumultuous. Perhaps, when we lit into poor Bill in October, we were already on edge. As you can guess, over the last three months, each of us has characterized the debacle in our own fashion.

**Jerry:** This has to be the worst crisis in the history of the Republic.

**Bob (me):** Didn't we say the same thing during the Vietnam War? And how about 1789? 1863?

**Evan:** "White House?" Where this loser really belongs is the Big House—maybe, the Nut House.

**Joan:** Actually, he lost by 2.9 million votes.

**Charlotte:** Any decent candidate could have wiped the floor with either of the ones that ran.

**Bill:** The whole business boggles the mind.

**Bob (me—to myself):** The uncivil, possibly irrelevant way we had jumped on Bill's slip-up in October may have prefigured our current behavior: as good liberals, we seem more interested in in-fighting than in getting anything done. We've also become hypersensitive to fake news.

* * *

ON ANOTHER NOTE, just last week, I had coffee with Evan. Not that he and I are soul mates, or anything, but he sent me a text message imploring me to meet him, which I translated as: "Hey, Bob, need your wise counsel. Can we meet for a coffee, please? You name place and time, but ASAP! *Gracias*, Ev."

Since I'm a childless widower, and retired (from high-school teaching), I do have plenty of free time.

> *"Time, time," said old King Tut,*
> *"is one thing I've got nothing but."*

So I emailed my acceptance, and the next morning Evan and I met at a local coffee shop. This place is an oasis, where people work so quietly on their laptops and other devices that conversation is possible. The coffee shop is this senior's default place for tranquil proximity. Nowadays, the public library has too many ranting homeless and/or mentally ill, not to mention the librarians, who chatter away loudly and incessantly. I bet that, instead of vows of silence, even the strictest cloisters post notices now, requesting that the acolytes "Please Keep Your Voices Down."

After Evan had paid for my small regular and his cheese Danish and latté, and when we were ensconced (that word, again) in a back corner, he went straight to the point. I listened without interrupting.

"I swear, Bob, I'm losing it. All this rich white trash is moving into my building. They've taken over the Board, and their 'improvements' are driving maintenance through the roof. I mean, I love my apartment, but I've reached the absolute ceiling of what I can pay." (Were the building metaphors a joke?) He went on in that vein, for a while, complaining about things like a chandelier and new marble paneling in the lobby.

Like many other young New Yorkers, Evan runs a small tech start-up. Don't quote me, but I think they provide software systems to banks to help streamline their taxes, or something. He may even have one or two employees. The relevant point is that his current "income stream," as he complained, was "a trickle," and that he was overdrawn at (yes) his own bank.

Was I sympathetic? Well, yes. Evan is a congenial young man, relatively polite, even bookish, in our culture of gadget-driven illiteracy and free-flowing rudeness. He's also a faithful member of the book club: always on time, does the reading, brings good cannoli. On the other hand, isn't his business exactly the kind of thing that drove millions of Americans to vote for The Great Satan in November? And they had a point: not only are tech jobs replacing manufacturing jobs, but Evan's company services the robber banks. Not to mention that his "problem" might seem like a mild, well-deserved indisposition for a member of the urban elite, at least in the eyes of stern judges in the heartland, and the poor (working or not) elsewhere, many of whom are struggling with substance abuse or terminal illness.

But, focusing on his good points, what advice did I offer? "I see your problem, Evan," I said. (Some idiots might have said, "I feel your pain.") "And I can think of two obvious ways out of it. The first would be to sell your apartment and move to a less expensive part of town. I'm sure the rich white trash in your building—I like that phrase—have already created a fair amount of 'enhanced property value,' so you may be sitting on a valuable piece of real estate. Second option: go into arrears on the maintenance until you get your next big contract, then use the money to catch up."

"But what would *you* do, Bob?"

"Sorry, Ev. I'm not you, am I? Think about it. I'm retired, on a fixed income, and too old to move."

"But what would you do if you *were* me?" I admire persistence, which can be the congenial obverse of rudeness.

"Okay, Evan, since you insist, I'll fall back on the old Socratic injunction: 'Know Thyself.' How much is your maintenance? What prospects are in the pipeline for your business? How wedded are you to the neighborhood? Do you have a partner whose needs you have to consult?" (I wish I still had one, myself.)

"Shit, Bob," he said. "How come I'm paying you the big consultant bucks?" Evan can be droll.

But so can I—or, at least, I try. "Excuse me, young man, but was that 'big consultant bucks' a fat joke? And, assuming it was, it doesn't apply. I may have shrunk to 5'7", by now, but I've also shrunk to 135." Evan is a gangly youth, bearing some resemblance to the cartoon character, Goofy.

The meeting ended with a surprise. Out on the sidewalk, when I extended my hand, he ignored it, clasping me, instead, to his bosom. As he grabbed me, he offered an explanation. "Hey, Bob, I go high." From the context, this must be a slang term for a "man hug." Or was he quoting our beloved former First Lady?

✳ ✳ ✳

LAST WEEK, LOOKING back at our October texts, I found further parallels to the current situation. I reread in Bottomsley, for example, that, "At the beginning, there were no inhabitants on the island." Then, they came, in waves, as it were (by water—no land bridges): the Neolithic, the Sicani, Sicels, Elymians, Greeks, Romans, Byzantines, Arabs, Normans, Hohenstaufens, Aragonese, etc. What would Sicily be without its immigrants? What would *we* be?

We're all set for next week's meeting. Jerry is bringing his cheesecake (store-bought, low-fat), and the text we have chosen (at the *O'Oh* meeting last month) is Thucydides' *The Peloponnesian War* (David Grene, transl.). These days, in search of ways out of our mess, everyone seems to be rereading: Orwell, Mill, Plato—you name it. We thought we were being original with Thucydides, but even that hoary tome seems to be on its way to the bestseller lists.

I can anticipate the gist of our discussion. An eloquent, democratic leader (Pericles/Obama) is undone by imperial entanglements (Athenian Empire/Middle-Eastern wars), and by economic issues (Athens goes broke/technology drops American manufacturing in the toilet). And the rest, as they say, is history—politics, actually. Or, as one Thucydides website puts it:

"His strategies were quickly abandoned, and the leaders who followed lacked Pericles' foresight and forbearance, instead committing even the conduct of state affairs to the whims of the multitude."[22]

Or, as Evan might say, we're in deep shit.

## The End

---

[22] Thucydides, *The Peloponnesian War*, trans. Rex Warner (Harmondsworth, UK, Penguin Books, 1972)

IF THAT KIND of progressive hair-splitting falls short, perhaps magic can dig us out of the "deep shit."

## The Dictator Confronted by The Magus

"HOW THE HELL did you get in here?" The Dictator groped for the buzzer beneath his desk, almost pressing the red nuclear button instead.

"Don't bother," said the intruder, a tall man dressed in the gray hooded robe of a Dominican friar. "It isn't working. Besides, I'm not here to harm you. My purpose is to try to lift the cloud of unknowing in which you grope out your days."

"'Cloud of... *what?* Who the hell are you?" demanded the Dictator, rubbing his bald head. "And who sent you?"

"I am sure you have never heard of me," he said. "My name is Giordano Bruno da Nola.[23] In life, I was a Magus."

The visitor seemed aware of the perhaps counterintuitive fact that listening was a skill many dictators seem to possess in abundance. After all, over the six long years leading up to February 17th, 1600, he had endured hundreds of interminable colloquies with his Inquisitors, at which point they had burned him at the stake—without even the usual courtesy of prior strangulation.[24]

---

[23] "da Nola," refers to Bruno's origins in the small town of that name, in the shadows of Mount Vesuvius (https://www.britannica.com/biography/Giordano-Bruno).

[24] www.historytoday.com/richard-cavendish/giordano-bruno-executed

# "Giordano Bruno, Biography, Death & Facts"

"As for your other question," he continued, "the answer is complex. I suppose you could say History sent me, or the Universe. Not Hell, though, I don't believe in Hell." With that, he drew back his cowl, revealing a stern, weathered face with a grizzled mustache and mad, glittering eyes.

Swinging his black boots onto his polished desk, and slouching down on his ergonomic throne, the unfazed Dictator fingered the gold buttons of his black military tunic. "Yeah, right, you're a messenger from History and the Universe. Can I see your credentials? And I'm the Pope." He thought for a nanosecond. "Hmm," he muttered. "Not a bad idea. I'll have to look into that."

Bruno frowned at this unconsciously insensitive reference to his chief tormentor. Without inviting him to sit in the smaller chair on the far side of the desk, the Dictator glanced at his gold wristwatch. "You've got thirty seconds, pal, before I throw you out…" He remembered the dead buzzer. "…even if I have to do it personally."

Bruno responded to this threat by passing a hand through the top of the desk, a silent demonstration of his incorporeality. The Dictator's mouth fell open, and the air seemed to go out of his bulky frame. The Magus snapped his fingers, causing the Dictator's red sash to snap painfully against his chest, like a big rubber band.

"Stop blustering and listen to what I have to say."

A deep furrow appeared in the Dictator's brow. Had he really threatened to throw this intimidating intruder out? "Okay, shoot," he said, forming an imaginary pistol with the thumb and forefinger of his right hand. "But make it quick, I'm a busy man."

"As for me, I have all the time in the world—and beyond this world." Drawing himself up to his full height, and aiming a forefinger at the Dictator, the Magus chanted, "In the name of Sol, the one true god, and his attending spirits, including Isis, divine Sophia, the celestial spheres and terrestrial animals, and the decans and constellations of the sub-Jovian world, I, Giordano Bruno da Nola, do hereby declare that, unless you immediately cease and desist from stoking hatred among your fellows, in the interests of battening your larcenous ego, you will be consigned forever to historical oblivion."

The Dictator pretended to be frightened. "Ooh," he mocked, "'historical oblivion.' As long as they don't forget me."

Bruno shrugged, and silently pointed to the Dictator's smart phone, which sat on a corner of the desk, looking like a turquoise postage stamp on an enormous brown envelope. Lunging for the device, and clicking it awake, instead of the usual welter of adulation, the Dictator saw that, except for four words, the screen was empty:

## YOU HAVE BEEN DELETED

"Hey, let's make a deal," he squeaked. "Wow! I bet I could delete all my enemies. Could you teach me how to do that? I mean, I'm pretty...what's that word...charismatical, myself."

"What you just witnessed was nothing like your so-called charisma. Yours is an evil magic; mine, a benevolent."

"Yeah, right. That's what they all say."

✶ ✶ ✶

AT THAT MOMENT, the door sprang open, and the Advisor, a heavyset, arrogant-looking man with curly brownish-gray hair, strode into the room. He wore thick glasses and a tweed jacket with leather elbow patches.

"Don't you knock, anymore?" scolded the Dictator.

The Advisor ignored both the complaint and the visitor. "Sign this," he commanded. "It might undo some of the damage your recent outbursts have done to our alliances." He sailed a single sheet of paper across the desk.

"Aren't you even going to ask who my visitor is? He's a holy man who does magic tricks. Calls himself 'Señor Bruno.'"

"*Signor* Bruno," the Magus corrected.

Other than a cursory nod, the Advisor ignored the oddly dressed visitor, who did not look anything like a member of the evangelical contingents he often encountered in this office. "Just sign," he repeated.

The Dictator drew his fountain pen from its gilt holder and flourished it, in preparation for signing the document. As the Advisor waited, he peered owlishly at Bruno. "A magician, eh? Maybe, you could use a spell to undo some of the damage this moron causes every day." The Dictator opened his mouth to protest, but a stern glance from the Advisor made him shut it. "Maybe, you could even restore his wits—not that he ever had any."

"Hey!" protested the Dictator.

"'Therein, the patient must minister to himself,'" quoted the Magus.

"*Macbeth*, Act 5, Scene 3, lines 48 to 49," said the Advisor.

"Ah, I see you are an educated man."

"He knows everything," boasted the Dictator, whose pen was still circling the document like a plane waiting to land at a busy airport.

Addressing the Advisor, the Magus said, "Presumably, then, sir, you have read my thirty-second book. Written in Switzerland, and published in Frankfort, the title, as you will recall, is *De Imaginum, Signorum et Idearum Compositione*."

Vain about his knowledge, the Advisor replied, "Why, yes, I believe I have read that one. The date was around 1590, wasn't it?" Cognizant of the general outlines of Bruno's biography, he was guessing.

"1591. But, since you have, indeed, read the book, I find it astonishing that you can continue to serve such a master."

"Eh?"

"As you will recall, in one illustration, Jupiter, the First Principle of the Universe, is standing in a chariot. Arrayed on his left hand are figures representing Pride, Display, Ambition, Dementia, Vanity, Contempt For Others, and Usurpation; and, on his right, Life, Incorrupt Innocence, Erect Integrity, Clemency, Hilarity, Moderation, and Toleration. Well, then, sir?"

"Eh?" repeated the Advisor.

"It seems to me that the figures on the left precisely describe your master; those on the right, everything he spurns. *Ergo?*"

For a moment, the Advisor seemed stunned by the Magus' argument. But, never at a loss, he sprang to the counterattack.

## Continuation of the Dialogue between the Advisor and the Magus

**Advisor:** What can I say? We're not in the Sixteenth Century, anymore, Toto.

**Magus:** "*Toto,*" you call me? "All"? Well, yes, I suppose I am.

**A:** Never mind, that was a joke—after your time. What I mean is, ours is a complicated world, full of frightening conflicts.

**M:** Was my world so different, torn as it was by doctrinal strife stoked by self-interest and demagoguery? But my magic offered a solution. If things had only gone…differently, all those terrible religious and dynastic wars could have been curtailed.

**A:** "If!" A *compadre* of yours, Tommaso Campanella, did catch the ear of Cardinal Richelieu, and your sun worship had its day in—at—court. The results were the absolutism of Louis XIV, and the French revolution.

**M:** I regret those unfortunate developments.

**A:** Anyway, wasn't that one-world cosmology business originally cooked up by your predecessor, Marcilio Ficino, to cure rampant depression, then called "melancholia," among his students? Your "magic" was a bunch of mumbo-jumbo designed for the couch. More like cosmetology than cosmology.

**M:** Not only is depression ubiquitous among the youth of today, but your allusion to Ficino is a foolish quibble. You surely know enough about the history of technology to be aware that numerous inventions designed for specific purposes—in many instances, for war—have been adapted to wider, more benevolent uses. Is this not the case, for example, with those thinking machines everyone today seems to worship?

**A:** Computers?

**M:** Besides, what do you offer in place of my one-world "cosmetology?"

**A:** Well, to put it in terms that will be familiar, my boss and I are like the lion and the fox. He threatens; I negotiate. It's about leverage. Or, as Ludwig von Rochau put it, three or four hundred years after Machiavelli, we practice *realpolitik*. Besides, in recent times, we've tried that one-world stuff again. Since you seem to be so well informed, I'm sure you've heard of the League of Nations and its successor, the United Nations. The League failed dismally to prevent World War Two, and, ever since, the U.N. has been impotent in the face of global carnage.

**M:** There has always been carnage, and we have always had lions and foxes. But, nowadays, humanity faces a new and uniquely serious threat. Five centuries after my death, the alchemy of money and ignorance has come to dominate human affairs more completely than ever before, and this toxic mix is fast destroying Nature, which I value above all else. Your master, who should be a bulwark against this calamity, is, instead, its aggressive agent.

* * *

BEFORE THE ADVISOR could reply, the Dictator, who had been watching the exchange as if it were a tennis match, finally piped up. "Yadda, yadda," he sneered. "No wonder the Inquisition burnt your crazy ass."

Instead of replying, the Magus drew back the sleeves of his robe, made a circular motion with his arms, and intoned an ancient Egyptian spell. Suddenly, the room was filled with dazzling golden light, in which danced a swarm of gorgeous visions, including planetary bodies, the atmospheric forces of wind, rain, thunder, and lightning, representatives of the animal, vegetable, and mineral kingdoms, and emblems of gods and goddesses from both the Egyptian and Greek pantheons.[25]

Even the Advisor seemed impressed, and the expression on the open-mouthed Dictator's face was that of a child opening hitherto unimagined Christmas presents. Within a few moments, however, the magical figures had faded and disappeared, as had the Magus.

"Where'd he go? Spontaneous combustion," quipped the Dictator.

"There's no such thing. Sign the paper."

---

[25] Yates, Frances, *Giordano Bruno and the Hermetic Tradition* (Chicago, The University of Chicago Press, 1964; Midway reprint, 1979).

118

As the Dictator once again flourished his pen, he was heard to murmur, "But I *like* elephants."

## The End

# IV. FAMILIES (1): SURROGATE



"They hate us youth!"[26]

AS A FIRST, and perhaps unusual, take on surrogate families, I offer this scientific and philosophical fable of the frantic efforts of an eccentric to conquer mortality. Although his age is seven years short of Gravy (63), he belongs to the legions of the old at heart.

## Living in the Moment

IN THE FULLNESS of time, Mr. Cucire developed a peculiar delusion: that he would live longer by breaking things into their smallest units. Instead of walking across a room, for example, he would flex his left foot, extend it, and so on. Shopping? Cooking? Eating? Don't ask.

In the fullness of time, as well, there must have been someone (or ones) else who had experienced this particular delusion. Has anything happened once? Yes, of course: he, himself, had been born once, and he would die once. How many discrete moments would pass before that latter singularity? For that matter, would any or all of those moments be singular? Well, of course, yes and no.

One moment, early one morning, one Sunday, late one winter, Mr. Cucire stood on the sidewalk in front of his house preparing to extend his foot. He noted the bright sunshine and the absence of snow, none having fallen that year. He also noted that, along the front fringe of his neighbor's lawn, a few flowers, such as scarlet sage (or *Salvia splendens*, an annual, in the north, but a perennial, in its native Brazil), stubbornly hung on.

---

[26] Falstaff, speaking to Prince Hal, Shakespeare, *I Henry IV*, 2.2.9

A little girl came walking toward him from the corner, chanting the old adage, "Step on a crack." In her own way, she trod as carefully as he did. Raising his head at the sound of her approach, Mr. Cucire focused his eyes, perceived her presence, identified the chant, observed the way she took a little hop-step at every crack, and thought to himself, "A kindred soul."

"Oh, oh," thought the little girl, "that looks like the kind of man Mom told me to watch out for." ("Avoid," Mom had meant.)

Since it was a very quiet morning, and she did not hear the sound of any approaching vehicle, she swerved toward the curb and hopped off, intending to cross the street so she would not have to pass the strange man. As she did so, a silent sports car with a drunken driver careened around a corner a block-and-a-half behind her and, turning east directly into the low sun, zoomed straight toward her. She froze.

Mr. Cucire was faced with a dilemma that required immediate attention. He knew he should watch out for (protect) the girl, so he considered whether to shout a warning, rush into the street and physically remove her from harm's (the car's) way, or both. If Mr. Cucire was going to shout, he must do so without first deciding to open his mouth, draw a deep breath, and so on. Even so, a shout might not cause the girl to move out of the car's path, and by now it might also be too late to take the steps requisite to rushing out. So, almost simultaneously, he opened his mouth, shouted, flexed his leg muscles, leapt into the street, and with a single motion of his outstretched arm, swept the startled girl back onto the sidewalk, where she landed on her bottom. A moment later, the car passed, a blur of careless speed.

Mr. Cucire sighed. The frightened little girl, a tear running down her cheek, managed a brave smile. "Thank you for saving me, mister," she said.

Extending an arm, Mr. Cucire helped the girl to her feet. As he clasped the small hand in his, without even realizing it, I—yes, *I*—became a new man. For my notion of living in the moment had undergone an instantaneous change that, in its own way, was as cosmic as that cataclysmic moment in the history of our cosmos, the Big Bang

In the weeks that followed my Big Bang moment, however, I (Mr. Cucire) discovered that being a new man was no simple…matter. Perhaps, I was naïve not to have anticipated difficulties.

One way to explain what happened is to say that half of me became a toddler. My adult brain, that is, seemed trapped inside a toddler's hyperactive, hyperkinetic body. Previously, living in the moment had meant living in a hermetic world of micro-motion driven by micro-decisions. Should I stretch out my foot? Stretch, or don't. Should I flex my knee? Flex, or don't. Now it—Living in the Moment, or LITM—meant having to negotiate a, yes, exhilarating—but complex and undifferentiated—whirl. I was still bombarded with constant choices, but—how to say this?—the choices were bundled.

Should I see a movie? Okay. What should I have for dinner? Fish. Will the fish market still be open when the movie ends? Check the running time in the paper and call the market. Is it walking distance from the theater? Yes. But will I have time? Easily.

Having figured all that out in less than a minute, I'm off to the movies, ten blocks away, conscious of hurrying past one block, then another, thinking of six other things as I rush along. Type of fish? Popcorn? Pay the bills? Call the eye doctor? My life was like a meteor shower. It appeared that the automatic act of rescuing a little girl had plunged me into a world of spontaneity and simultaneity.

The phone rings. What I, the adult, must do in one complex act is to decide whether to answer, or to let the machine pick up, and, assuming the former, prepare myself as I cross the room for whomever it might be; or, if the latter, and if the caller should turn out to be someone with whom I wish to speak, decide whether to cross the room so I can pick up, after all…and so on.

Had I been an actual toddler left alone in the room with the ringing telephone, my reaction would have been virtually automatic. I would have toddled across the floor, and assuming no one else was present or ran in to stop me, that nothing else diverted me, and that the phone cord was within my reach, I would probably have yanked it, bringing the phone crashing to the ground, after which I would have grabbed the receiver and, seated on the floor, said calmly and rationally, "Herro. Who is dis?"

Answering the phone is such a simple act. Shopping, socializing, reading, listening, watching, going, returning…not to mention playing the larger roles: citizen, thinker, friend (I still had a few), and (dare I hope again? some day?) lover…for a man like me, at my age, sixty-three, all these roles and requisite behaviors made for an exhausting round. Like Dickens' Dr. Manette, I had been "recalled to life." But like him, too, or like nuns or priests who leave their cloisters, or any other released long-term prisoner, I found it very difficult to wean myself from the hermetic micro-world of my recent past.

Fairly soon, I realized that I needed, in modern parlance, "to get help." But, characteristically, for me "help" meant rational understanding. So I decided to speak not to a mental health professional, but to a philosopher. (Not to boast, but back in my salad days, a professor of philosophy had commented at the bottom of a paper for which he gave me an A-, "You show real aptitude for this discipline.") Luckily, many philosophers love to talk, and, luckily, too, I had a notion of how to get access to one.

So, in the midst of a morning's meteor shower (eat breakfast, use the bathroom, get dressed, go shopping, put away the perishables, turn on the computer, pay the bills), I emailed a niece who was, herself, an academic, but in a distant town. Having received prompt and positive replies from her and, subsequently, from the colleague she selected, one morning a few days ago, I took two buses across town to the campus of Pergament College where I found my way to his office.

To backtrack for a moment, this was the first email exchange:

Hello, Stephanie,

I'm sorry I've been out of touch so long, and I hope you won't think too badly of me if I confess that my motive for resuming contact is to ask a favor. Put simply, I wonder if you happen to know of a philosopher in or near Pergament. The simplest way to explain this request is to say that I've undergone an existential crisis. Not a breakdown, or anything—please don't worry—but a change of life that I would like to understand in rational, even abstract, terms.

Given this desire, if I may compound the request, I think a generalist would be best, someone who knows the literature and can help me sort out Thales from Heraclitus, Locke from Hume, and Charles S. Peirce from William James. Finally—and this may seem quixotic—I would prefer someone who is detached and neutral enough *not* to lecture me that Plato is infinitely superior to Aristotle, or Derrida, to somebody else, or any other such nonsense.

I hope this message finds you and yours well. Please give my best to any other members of our family with whom you may be in touch, and assure them that my protracted silence implies no judgment, whatsoever, of them.

Thank you very much, dear niece, for any help you may be able to offer.

With warm wishes,
I. Cucire.


Dear Uncle Irwin,

My, my, after all these years! How wonderful to hear from you! I certainly remember the fun we used to have when I was a girl of eight or nine, and you were my funny old bachelor uncle. Weren't you the one who used to pull quarters out of my ears? As you must imagine, I've often wondered what became of you, and it's good to know that you are not only alive, but that you sound very well or, at least, in control of your faculties.

I think I may have just the person you need. Jack Taylor was my husband Bob's and my instructor in a wonderful History of Philosophy course way back when. Jack now teaches part-time at Pergament College, and since he's an Emeritus, I'm confident he'll have time to talk with you. His age is probably an advantage in another way, too: Professor Taylor was trained during an era when philosophers were still expected to be familiar with all the major schools, and when the subject was taught as objectively as possible, without the distorting lenses of Structuralism, Post-Structuralism, Deconstructionism, Post-Colonialism, Gender and Ethnic Studies, and all the other new approaches that—dare I say?—currently dog the training and careers of nascent academics in all branches of what Bob and I refer to as "the illiberal arts."

Anyway, here is the contact information: jotaylor@pergament.edu. Please mention that I suggested you get in touch with him and do give him our very best wishes. (I hope he remembers us.)

As for me—where to begin? Married, two children, tenured, Bob, likewise, mom (your sister) still alive (mild Alzheimer's), but dad died c. four years ago. And, yes, Irwin, dear, I will certainly pass along your greetings to the rest of the family. If you like, I can even send you some news about them.

I'd be interested to hear how your interview with Jack goes. The little you told me about your motive sounds fascinating. But you can tell me more later, or not, as you choose, dear Uncle. Good to be back in touch.


With all warm wishes,
Steph


✳ ✳ ✳


WELL, THAT WAS so generous and straightforward that it made me rethink the question of why I had isolated myself for all those years. Frankly, the possibility of acceding to Stephanie's tactful suggestion of renewed family relations did appeal, but, to paraphrase an old college joke, that seemed as if it would be putting Descartes (the cart) before Horace (the horse). Not to mention that, for me, opening up the past would probably be something like inviting a recurrence of Hayley's Comet. So I sent her my thanks, made the contact, received a prompt, affirmative reply, and, on the appointed morning, was off to see the philosopher.

I'll skip that day's meteor shower, limiting myself to a hurried account of the preliminaries: the newly budding campus (spring just cresting the horizon: lilies, daffodils, nasturtiums, and *Centaurea cyanus*, or bachelor's button); the old-fashioned, cluttered, top-floor corner office in the modern glass tower,

126

belonging—according to the wooden plaque on the door—to "Professor John. M. Taylor," a tall, thin, wrinkled, and genial old man in a tweed jacket with leather elbow patches, long, straight white hair (no facial), and, perhaps in a concession to modern medicine, no pipe.

"Well, Mr. Cucire," said the Professor when we had introduced ourselves and settled into the comfortable red leather club chairs, catty-cornered to each other in front of his desk. "What can I do for you?"

"Thank you for seeing me, Professor Taylor. I realize this is an unorthodox request."

* * *

IN THE INTEREST of conciseness, I will present the rest of our discussion in dialogue form, without descriptive, narrative, or astronomical interruptions. As a shortcut, readers may themselves insert a variety of gestures, facial expressions, and tones of voice: on his part, steepling of fingers, scratching of chin, nods, and smiles, often quizzical; on mine, grimaces, throat clearing, arms spread, palms upward, head-scratching, and rubbing. I will also skip the conversational preliminaries regarding my niece and her husband, Bob, constrained, of course, by a forty-year family hiatus, not to mention my never having laid eyes on Bob. And, finally, I will conclude this preface to the dialogue by saying that the professor asked first whether he could assume familiarity, on my part, with the basic tenets of the best-known philosophical traditions. My reply was that, allowing for mistakes, a poor memory (false modesty), and superficiality, which I hoped he would excuse, he could so assume.

**JT:** So. Your email said you wanted some philosophical perspectives on a personal problem. I assume you're not interested exclusively in the school of Humanistic Psychology—Rollo May, Erich Fromm, *et alia?*

**IC:** Correct. I want to see a personal situation through a variety of philosophical lenses.

**JT:** Excellent. You called your situation "an existential crisis." Would you elaborate?

(I outlined the two incarnations of LITM, including the watershed incident with the little girl, but not the tortuous and murky series of events leading to the first incarnation.)

**JT:** I assume you've skipped over the etiology of LITM-One—shall we call it that?—because you want to steer me away not only from Humanistic Psychology, but from the psychological aspects of other schools. If I may say so, we will need very skillful navigation if we are to avoid those reefs and shoals, and still reach the promised land of some serious answers to your questions.

**IC:** Don't worry, I expect rough sledding—sailing.

**JT:** Good. Even so, perhaps we should use as our starting point your own designation, Existentialism, which is, alas, a school of thought firmly anchored in psychology, not to mention the other social sciences.

**IC:** Yes. I know that. Shoot!

**JT:** I would suggest that LITM-One quite neatly qualifies you as an Existentialist. I hope you don't mind being pigeonholed, but LITM-One was—is—a way of facing existence without relying on prearranged categories. You would gain the praise of Sartre, Camus, and the other non-religious Existentialists for your implied refusal to live your life according to the dictates of prefabricated, unquestioned ideologies, many of which—principally imperialism, religion, and capitalism— operate in the service of oppression by the *salauds*, or "bastards".

**IC:** That sounds good. Correct me if I'm wrong, but when I saved the girl and shifted to LITM-Two, I experienced an existential moment, performing an act of *engagement?*

**JT:** Approximately. Of course, even after that act, the universe remained random, or *absurde*, to you, and you did not embark upon a course of serving others, like a doctor in a time of plague, or a member of the Resistance. But, perhaps, even as we speak, you're on your way.

**IC:** I wouldn't bet on it. Excuse me, but that analysis sounds so glib, so…puerile.

**JT:** It does, doesn't it? That's exactly the criticism the Positivists made of their opposite numbers across the Channel: complete lack of rigor. As you may also know, more profane, lay persons, have called the Existentialists everything from "Curly Fries" to "Shitface."

**IC:** I didn't know that. But it must be time to move on.

**JT:** To Positivism, then? Do you want to look next at the implications for LITM of language, logic, and mathematics?

**IC:** That sounds difficult and dry. Can I take a rain check?

**JT:** Well…okay. But someone has given you bum scoop, you know. How about a few tidbits, at least?

**IC:** Oh, all right. Shoot!

**JT:** For instance, do past and future objects exist in the same sense, ontologically speaking, as present ones do? And, after all, most linguists call the present and the past, "tenses," but the future, an "aspect"—i.e. only hypothetical. Is tonight's supper the same as this morning's breakfast?

**IC:** Well, I wasn't planning to eat the same thing, but…

**JT:** Ha, ha! Put more technically, do spatiotemporal objects like you and me exist by having temporal parts in much the same way as we have spatial ones, so that only "part" of us exists at any moment? And then there's that oldie, but goodie, time travel: could I go back in time and kill my own paternal grandfather before my father was born, and, if not, why not?

**IC:** Hmm, there's a thought. Was it the same me as the present me who used to flex his knee, then extend it? Do both LITMs negate the future? Could I go back and let that car hit the little girl? (Not that I'd want to, of course, but we *are* being academic here.) But "Hold! Enough!" Can we move on?

**JT:** Good questions. *Macbeth*, Act Five, Scene Eight. Why not? Suppose I bang out a few softballs. How about the pre-Socratics?

**IC:** Now you're talking.

(For the gist of the next phase of our discussion, I refer the reader to the opening of this narrative, with the addition of nametags: Thales, Heraclitus, and Plato's dialogue, *The Parmenides*.)

**JT:** Had enough of the Pre-Socs? They don't really reach any conclusions, do they? They just veer off into physics and math. Suppose we skip the Scholastics, too. If we start talking about God—*that* God—we'll never get anywhere. Let's just say He wants you to live in the moment, since He created all of the moments. But He also wants you to live as if you were a free agent, and He wants you to see the Big Picture, realizing that the moment is only significant as it leads to your latter end—after you die, that is. In my opinion, all of those mandates add up to a tall, incompatible order. So. Next?

**IC:** Let's do Hume. I always liked him.

**JT:** Well, actually, Hume was reacting to Thomistic philosophy, wasn't he? Are you familiar with the question of form and *esse*?

**IC:** I seem to remember it from college, but only "as through a beer glass darkly."

**JT:** Ha, ha! *First Corinthians*. Anyway, let's talk about those celebrated billiard balls. If we posit two things that, for practical purposes, are identical, like billiard balls, we can talk about efficient causality.[27] By that, I mean…[Phone rings.] Oh, shit, I forgot. It must be my daughter, she's about to have a baby. Can we…?

Barely avoiding knocking it off his desk, Professor Taylor grabs the phone. ("Hel-*lo?*") With profuse, murmured thanks, I whisper loudly that the rest can wait, that I'll be in touch in a week or two. As I tiptoe from the office, closing the door behind me, I hear a muffled shout: "A boy? Wonderful! Details, please."

* * *

BY NOW, TWO months later, everything has shifted again, and my contact with the old philosopher has yet to be resumed. In fact, it is an open question whether it ever will. Life, it seems, has once again intruded. Heraclitus *triumphans!* This is what happened.

A few days after the colloquy, I am once again out on the sidewalk in front of my house. Early morning, and I am being serenaded by the bright, lusty chorus of the annuals of spring (you name them), not to mention the perennials (e.g., *Caryopteris* Dark Night). Along the sidewalk, out of the west, just like the first time, comes that little girl. But now she is holding the hand of an also pleasant-looking, forty-something woman. (Further details available upon request.) Freeze. The little girl points her finger; the woman smiles, and waves her free hand in my direction. My urge to turn and hightail it back into the house manifests itself in a presumably imperceptible twitch.

"Excuse me? Sir?"

"Yes?"

We move forward; she fast, I, slowly.

---

[27] Lawrence Dewan, "Form and Being: Studies in Thomistic Metaphysics," *Studies in Philosophy and the History of Philosophy* (2006).

"I'm so glad we ran into [ahem] you. I wanted to thank..."

The rest may be inferred. Suffice it to say that a crucial sequence of events has since transpired, involving, no doubt, an infinite number of discrete thoughts, impulses and actions, whether processed as in a Cuisinart, or not.

"How many?" you insist.

Who's counting? Although this may require a leap of faith, suffice it to say that I am about to become, literally, *engaged.* Whether this development will, in turn, hurl me back into LITM-One, allow me to carry on with LITM-Two, or bring me to some hitherto unimagined amalgam ($LITM^{1.5}$), or even to a completely new mode ($LITM^n$), Time will, or will not, tell.[28]

## The End

---

[28] Consultations with Peter Yamin (Physics), who suggested I read Steven Weinberg's *The First Three Minutes;* and with Dean Chapman and Brad Wolchansky (Philosophy). Brad directed me to a discussion of philosophical issues related to time in *The Stanford Encyclopedia of Philosophy.*

http://plato.stanford.edu/entries/time/

FRIENDS, OF COURSE, are a familiar form of surrogate families. When a wise cousin of my wife's lost his own wife, he advised us that keeping up with our friendships would provide a hedge against the demise of either life partner.

### The Old Boy Lunch Club

...rarely convenes. It's a matter of time.
Although there are only four of us,
the others' lives are as busy as mine.

Our wards are feline, avian, canine,
plus grandchildren we babysit and fuss over.
All these wards eat up our time.

We do good works, as well; our souls are fine.
We ride the volunteer omnibus.
Our motto is, "The world's problems are mine."

"I was less busy before I retired,"
a mot, apropos of the four of us,
a cliché that ages like fine old wine.

Still, we manage to meet from time to time,
sharing coal-fired pizza, noodles with sauce.
We pass the food around: no "yours," no "mine."

As I enjoy the meal, I study their eyes.
A certain far-away look I notice.
I'm sure they see the same look in mine.
The meaning is obvious: So little time.

After that "feel good" fable and poem, I hope the reader will forgive me for something really nasty. The malice that informs the following story has been both lauded and excoriated by friends, family, editors, and reviewers alike.

## The Parents We Deserve (Part One)

AFTER WHAT SEEMED an eternity, it finally happened: they died. Paula's mother (87) went first, and, two months later, her dad (89) came tumbling after.

"Oh, Paul," she sniffed. "Now I'm an orphan, too."

"There, there, babe," he said with a smile, "we all gotta go sometime." And they began to talk about whether to sell the Palm Beach condo immediately or to rent it month-to-month while they considered their options. Three weeks later the magnificent property (two bedrooms, three baths, golf course view) was gone: a million seven. Which brought their share of the total estate (one sibling, after taxes) to a decent but not outrageous, $673,426.50.

Was it mere coincidence that their names, Paul (mergers) and Paula (acquisitions), were so similar? Hardly. A decade earlier, and about a month into the negotiations for what they would soon be jocularly calling their "non-hostile mutual takeover," the name question had popped up at an expensive restaurant.

The expert waiter, having finished serving the snails, and having opened the excellent bottle of *Pinot Egrigio* for both diners to taste and praise, glided off into the restaurant's dim recesses. The foreground music was loud and sexy: romantic.

"Paula and Paul," Paula said, reaching over to take Paul's hand.

Looking into her eyes he said, "Paul and Paula. It was meant to be."

"Yep. To love."

"To self-love."

Clinking glasses, they drank to that.

* * *

FOR THE FIRST year or so after the demise of their second, and last, set of parents, the "orphans" sailed along swimmingly. They earned (two salaries, two bonuses, 2.6), they spent, they exulted. Another year passed, passably.

* * *

"ACCORDING TO THE famed French philosopher, René des Shopping-Cartes," quipped Paula one mid-summer Saturday afternoon as they stood before the perfume counter of a fine department store, "*J'achete, donc je suis.*"

Paul smiled dutifully at the forced adage, but inwardly he frowned. Sucking in seven or eight fragrances with one big gasp, he held them in his lungs while his mind flashed to the connubial bottom line. Yes, he had to admit it: after eleven busy years, his wife's frequent wit, with its ambivalent edge, was finally getting to him. Not for the first, or even the second time, he knew in his heart that something was wrong with their relationship, that something was missing. And, as he finally exhaled, he knew exactly what that something was. Yes, it was time for the well-heeled, well-adjusted, thirty-something couple to have parents—again.

"Is it possible, P.? Do we really miss them?" Paula asked rhetorically. "The perpetual crises? The sense of entitlement? The demands? The immaturity?"

"You know we do," Paul replied. "Yes, it's irrational but, on some level, in some crazy way, all children need parents. Maybe it's just guilt, maybe it's a need to feel superior. Whatever. It's real."

So they agreed: they needed parents. And they needed them sooner, not later, since, after all, the biological clock was ticking and, in not too many years, Paul and Paula would be too old for the exacting task of "childing"—that is, of having parents.

But fortunately, as both of them also knew, it is the easiest thing in the world to buy love. Their ad ("Personals") in *Modern Immaturity*, that widely perused magazine for the target population, tempered a pound of bluntness with an ounce, at least, of tact:

Elderly couple wanted for full-time, live-in position as surrogate parents for financially secure, orphaned, thirty-something couple. Must be ambulatory, continent, able to assume position immediately.

Excellent salary/benefits, comfortable accommodations, plentiful food, usual parenting duties. Equal Opportunity employer. (No seniles, please.) Emails only: http://www.modim.com/pers#442/11

After two weeks, hundreds of applications, most of them unsuitable (including several pairs of overt perverts), and four interviews (negative), P&P finally found their couple. According to the terse e-application, Myron and Myrna (fearful symmetry) had just moved back to the city from (life is rich) Palm Beach, Florida.

This, the fifth and final interview, took place in the living room of Paul and Paula's split-level climate-controlled penthouse condo (three bedrooms, three baths). As the tan old couple sipped their "virgin" G&T's and tried not to succumb to the mixed nuts, Paul threw them an opening softball.

"So, then, folks, tell us why you're moving back to the city."

"Way too many old codgers just like us down there," Myron explained, gliding his loafers back and forth on the plush white carpet as if he were skiing while sitting down. "Then, there's the heat, the humidity. Whew! The travel brochures sure don't mention those things. May through October, the whole state is like a giant pizza oven. And we're the pepperoni."

P&P smiled politely as Myron pretended to pant and mop his brow. Myrna vigorously wagged her blue-rinsed head and flashed her Medicare-quality dentures, top and bottom.

"Pizza ovens are dry, not humid, dear," she corrected. "And how about the cost of living? There are so many millionaires down there we could hardly afford to buy our groceries and other necessities. And do you think they have senior-citizen discounts? Ha! Not on your life."

"Ha, ha," Myron said. "They have junior-citizen discounts. But that's enough complaining, dear. Don't mind Mother, folks, she's a great kidder. Speaking of kidding, did you hear the one about the rabbi and the alligator?" They hadn't, so he told it.

As soon as the mutual compliments had been completed and the door had closed softly behind the short, elderly couple, and after only a few snorts over their matching Wal-Mart golf outfits, Paul and Paula agreed that the search was over.

"Aren't they cute?" Paul said.

"Those are parents anyone could be ashamed of."

"Yes, they're exactly what we need."

It was true. Myron and Myrna appeared to be the quintessential parents: their sins seemed totally venial. Accordingly, the very next day, as per instructions, the Ps' white-shoe lawyer drew up a contract and, without hesitation, both couples inked said contract, money changed hands and, just like that, the Ps had hired the Ms. Two days later, furniture to follow, the old couple moved into the spacious guest bedroom, full bath attached, and cohabitation began.

* * *

IN SOME WAYS, the Ms gave excellent value for their generous salaries, perks, and allowances. Paul and Paula felt something like parental pride when a couple of middle-level managers from their office were practically rolling on the floor over Myrna's wonderful Victor Borgia imitation (she proved an accomplished piano hobbyist) and Myron's cascade of off-color limericks. The young couple was also gratified by the fact that M&M took an interest in the careers of "their" children. The new parents' quick grasp of the arcane machinations of modern high finance was a pleasant surprise.

Like any parent-child relationship, however, this one required adjustments on both sides. For instance, steps were quickly taken toward establishing a changed apartment routine. It was now fall, and every morning at eleven, while the maid cleaned their room and bath, the old couple would toddle off to a nearby park to watch the pre-school set cavorting in the playground. (Once, Myrna grabbed Myron's arm in the nick of time as he was lifting his leg to climb into the sandbox.)

There were, of course, the usual ailments endemic to second childhood—arthritis, lumbago, arrhythmia, dysphagia, dyspepsia, and so on—but, fortunately, the younger couple's generous health insurance plan included a rider for Medicare supplements.

Then there were the messes, which could have become serious bones of contention. During the first few dinners together, P&P would silently grieve and gnash their teeth at the distressingly frequent spills onto their priceless antique pink damask tablecloth.

"Maybe they can eat in the kitchen with the rest of the help," Paula ventured.

"No, no, dear. Dinner is a unique opportunity for quality family time." Four top-of-the-line plastic mats with a pattern based on Monet's water lilies brilliantly resolved the matter.

Toilet training (mess #2) was another potential deal-breaker. Myron was nearsighted, his stream spastic, and soon the maid was grumbling and making noises about quitting. But no sooner had the issue been tactfully raised than, without a bit of fuss, the old gentleman graciously agreed to do (all) his business sitting down, and the seat was permanently lowered.

Quick studies both, P&P readily consensed that they would have to do some proactive heavy lifting to keep the generation bridge in good repair. Towards the end of the first trimester, on a weekday evening when nothing else was on, they decided to pump a few hours into the family account. After they had batted around several non-starters, Paula came up with the perfect plan: they would take M&M to the movies, "to a (not too) exciting CG 75."

"Ha, ha, 'CG 75.' Good one, P," Paul allowed. "And we won't even have to talk to them."

"Not nice, P." Paula admonished. "Your own parents? Am I seeing the proverbial cloud no bigger than a man's middle finger here?" Paul inwardly frowned at this recidivism (double-barreled) on the part of his irrepressible other, who had not (seriously) lapsed since a wedding about a month before. On that occasion, having been assigned to a table with eight strangers as they picked their way through the mediocre catered meal, Paula had fired off (audible whisper) one of her polyglot specials:

"*Cavear emptat.*"

Meanwhile, back at the condo, finger pun ignored, the movie plan was broached. Myrna was "tickled," so dinner having been eaten and spilled, off they went.

"What are we seeing?" Myron asked, as they popped and crept into the cab.

"It's a surprise," said Paula.

"It's a great flick," Paul chimed in. "Trust me."

Myron, it must be said, looked as if he smelled a rat.

The movie was a revival, but, as Paul had observed, "Bet the ranch on it, they haven't seen this one." The proud young couple sat one row behind and to one side of their wards, both to allow them their independence and to watch and enjoy their reactions.

The now-classic film was as startlingly violent as P&P remembered it. At one point, the main character came across a severed ear, shown close-up and crawling with insects. A grinning Paul nudged Paula, for Myron and Myrna's jaws looked as if they had come unhinged, albeit, in Myron's case, because he was ingesting popcorn as fast as an industrial vacuum cleaner. When they got home, the family unit recapped their night out.

"Wow!" said Myron, doing his indoor skiing routine. "I haven't had that much fun since the *Scarface* remake. Remember the chainsaw behind the shower curtain?" Myrna, who was knitting a sweater for a grand (in both senses) niece, kept her counsel.

Later, P&P sat propped up on their huge pillows, stretched out on the gold satin bedspread of their ergonomic king-sized 9K Scandinavian bed, wearing their matching reading glasses, laptops humming in harmony (minor fifth). Looking up for a moment from the mega-merger (15.4 b) he was putting together, Paul observed, "Apparently, seventy-five percent of all participants in this evening's entertainment rate it a complete success."

"Check," Paula concurred, entering a (different) number into the report on the smallish hostile takeover (2.7 b) she was vetting. "Gangbusters."

* * *

AND SO IT went, a tissue of annoyances (many) and satisfactions (some). Then, sadly, twelve or thirteen weeks into the quasi-parent child relationship, as it reached what might be called its adolescence, the cloud grew huge and dark, then burst. As is so often the case, music proved the treacherous rock upon which the family vessel foundered. Both Ms were partially deaf; both passionately loved Mantovani and Lawrence Welk.

"A one-and-a-two-a," Paul quipped. "If they play that elevator shit one more time, it's bubbles in the cyanide for them."

And when the sensitive issue was broached, even though, after his homicidal private outburst, Paul did temper his language, the reaction was predictably oppositional.

"Darn it," Myron exploded, "can't we even listen to our own music? We never have any fun around here."

"That'll do, Myron," snapped Paul. "Go to your room. Now! Both of you."

Sulkily, with their blood pressures approaching dangerous levels but without another word, off the old couple trudged. Paul and Paula remained at the table. Trying to calm down, Paul twirled a leftover bread stick while Paula breathed deeply and stared into space.

A few minutes later, a thud was heard over the intercom. Its source was the guest bedroom, and it was immediately followed by a second thud. Paul and Paula stared at each other in wild surmise. Then, Paul groped for his cell.

* * *

AS IT TURNED out, two hearts that had beaten as one for half a century had stopped beating, almost as one. Two days later, Myron and Myrna were interred in a double box at a nearby cemetery. A top-of-the-line floral display (donors absent, anonymous) dominated the cortege.

141

The day of the funeral, after dinner, the couple (young) sat in silence in their matching red leather club chairs before the fire in their climate-controlled living room. After a few minutes, they both looked up.

"We're orphans again," Paula sighed.

"That's life, babe. It comes with the territory." He paused for a moment, maintaining eye contact. "Shall I, uh…?"

"Yes, please. Say something about 'musical tastes.'"

Popping his laptop, Paul booted up and cut and pasted the *Modern Immaturity* ad into a new one.

"How's this?" He read her the (revised) 2nd paragraph:

Excellent salary/benefits, comfortable accommodations, plentiful food, usual parenting duties, musical compatibility a must. Equal Opportunity employer. (No seniles, please.)

Emails only: http://www.modim.com/pers

"Send it," she said.

## The End

WHEN A GRAVY-ITE encounters a fellow member of our
fringe demographic, we sometimes exchange a furtive nod or a
word of complicity, something like the Boy Scout handshake:

## Brown, the Concept

An old boy toddles along the sidewalk
in busy conversation with himself.
Part of a burgeoning demographic,
he's too familiar for the young to notice.
But, as his co-old boy, I do notice…

On this cold day, he's almost all in brown:
boots, pants, coat, muffler, scarf, all the way up
to a watch cap, with "BROWN" in black letters.
Though a brown study, he's cheerful enough,
championing a young man's trendy color.

With that metonymic sign on his prow,
he could be a conceptual artist,
an ersatz semiologist, of sorts.
"Cold enough for you?" "Brown enough for you?

# V. FAMILIES (2): ACTUAL

"I think togetherness is a very important ingredient to family life."
–Barbara Bush[29]

DO YOU BELIEVE in coincidences? Without my even noticing it, the name of the dog in "Reader, I Read to Him" also turns up in this next story, "I, Muffin," as the name of the eponymous baked good. Co-authoring the story was my grandson, Leo Siegel, aged 6-7, at the time of writing. (I was 74-75.) "I, Muffin" serves as a transition from surrogate to actual families, since it contains both.

### (from I, Muffin, Part One)
### Chapter One: The Wacky Muffin

AN OLD WOMAN sitting on a bench in front of a bagel store accidentally dropped a muffin from a black plastic bag onto the sidewalk. This neighborhood was full of cafés, restaurants, bars, banks, chain drug stores, clothing boutiques, pet daycare centers, and nail spas. But no shoemakers, dry cleaners, supermarkets, barbershops, or thrift shops.

The woman, who did not look poor, stooped to pick up the muffin, barely preventing a second one from sliding from her bag. As she stooped, the fallen muffin began to speak.

---

[29] www.brainyquote.com/quotes/barbara_bush_383682

"Wait!" it said, in a gravelly voice. It was a golden-brown corn muffin, big and round, with cracks on top that resembled facial features (like the man in the moon). "What are you doing? Don't you realize what's on these sidewalks? Don't you know anything about germs?"

"Heavens!" exclaimed the round and pleasant-looking gray-haired woman, who was wearing glasses with plastic frames, a gray woolen coat, and shiny, new-looking orange and green running shoes. "A talking muffin." And, closing the bag, she began nervously brushing off the muffin.

"Who do you think you're fooling?" it asked, trying not to laugh because the brushing tickled. "You know you're not really getting the dirt off. And you don't even look poor."

The old woman became angry. "Mind your own business, you nosey…baked good." And she raised the muffin to her mouth.

But, before she could take a bite, it stopped her in her tracks. "Go ahead," it said. "Enjoy your filthy muffin."

This rude remark caused the woman to drop the muffin again. Leaving it on the sidewalk, she carefully pulled a second one from the bag, took a big bite, stood up, and hurried off.

But the new muffin was dry, and so (thanks to the first one's rude comment) was her mouth. So she put it back in the bag and walked on toward her apartment, two blocks south, where she intended to toast and eat the rest of her muffin, with raspberry jam, a nice cup of tea—and no more insults.

"My goodness," she thought, as she wove her way past big cracks in the sidewalk, people who were text messaging, and Sunday morning baby carriages and dog walkers. "It's getting so a person can't even enjoy the simple pleasures. Life has become so difficult."

Meanwhile, the clever muffin wasted no time. Before it could attract the attention of any of its natural enemies—bugs, pigeons, rats, squirrels, hungry homeless humans—it folded in its legs, flipped onto an edge, and, like a skillful skateboarder using its arms for balance, rolled north along the sidewalk toward its home, the little muffin room. This was a room behind the lobby of a famous old apartment house called The Bakery Building.

**Chapter Two: Muffin's Big Trick.**

IT WAS SPRING, and the weather was warmer. Out for a roll, Muffin saw the old woman walking in the park.

"Hi," he said. "There's a nice ice cream cart near here. Do you want to get some?"

"Well…o-kay." Although she had not forgotten his rudeness, he sounded friendly now. Besides, she loved ice cream.

So Muffin led the old woman to the cart, where she bought an orange Popsicle with vanilla ice cream. The vendor did not even ask Muffin what he wanted, because he could not see him on the ground in the shadow of the cart. The old woman sat down on a bench, with Muffin at her feet, and started to lick the delicious Popsicle. After a few moments, Muffin told her a riddle:

"Who do lions, tigers, and all the other animals hate to take tests with?"

"I don't know," she replied. "Who?"

"Cheetahs. Because they cheat."

"Ha, ha!" said the old woman. Shaking with laughter, she dropped a small piece of Popsicle on the toe of her shoe, and some more on Muffin. He rolled on the ground to wipe the ice cream off, and then ate the piece that had fallen on her shoe.

"Yummy," he said. "Thanks for the ice cream."

The old woman was angry. "The only reason," she said, "you told me that stupid riddle was so you could steal a taste of my ice cream."

Muffin did not reply. A golden-brown smile spread across his round face.

When she had finished the Popsicle, the old woman asked Muffin a question: "Tell me," she said. "How did you become so tricky?"

Muffin looked up at her, cleared his throat, and explained.

* * *

"THERE WAS ONCE a baker of muffins and bagels. Since he liked bagels much better, he would always bake at least twice as many bagels as muffins. I decided to teach him a lesson. One night, while he was asleep in his room behind the bakery, I crept up to his bed and gave him a bagel haircut. You know, I shaved off all the hair in the center, but left some around the edges.

"The next morning, the baker looked in the mirror and said, 'Hey, who's that bald guy? Yikes! It's me. My head looks like a...a bagel. Maybe this is just a dream.'

"With a big yawn, he went back to sleep. I crept back to the bed, dyed the baker's hair, and changed the style. When he woke up, refreshed from his extra sleep, he looked in the mirror again.

"'Wow,' he said. 'Look at that beautiful haircut!' His hair was now all even and golden in color, with the hair from the edges combed over the top to hide the bald spot. His head looked round and beautiful. 'Hey,' he said. 'My head looks like a muffin. Hmm, maybe, muffins aren't so...'"

Muffin smiled up at the old woman. "Hee, hee," he said, with a wink. "That day, the baker baked ninety-eight muffins and only two bagels."

"Well," said the old woman, "that was a clever trick. But I hope you won't play any more of your muffin tricks on me." And she gave him a sly look.

"Hmm," Muffin thought to himself, "I'd better watch out, or soon this old woman will be playing tricks on me."

## Chapter Three: Fox Shock

"HELLO? IS MR. Fox in?

"Speaking. May I help you?"

"Well, Mr. Fox, this is the old woman calling. I would like to invite you to a tea party at my house tomorrow."

"How nice. But it's summer, you know, and I'm pretty busy raiding chicken coops and stealing grapes from vineyards, so…"

"The other guest will be Muffin. I think you, er, like him."

"Whoa! Why, yes, in that case, I'll certainly be there. I'd love to eat…er, see my old friend, Muffin."

She hung up, then called Muffin and invited him, too.

"Hmm," said Muffin. "As long as you're not planning to serve bagels. Thanks. Who are the other guests?"

"Just one," the old woman replied. "It's a surprise, but you'll recognize him. He's an old friend…of mine."

"Hmm, okay," said Muffin. "What time?"

"Shall we say two-ish?"

"Two-ish, it is. See you then."

Muffin was suspicious. Opening his closet, he rummaged around until he found what he needed. The next day at two, when he arrived at the old woman's apartment, he was carrying a big black suitcase. Jumping up on the case, he pressed her buzzer.

"So glad to see you, Muffin," said the old woman. "Come in, the other guest is already here." She held the door open, but Muffin hesitated.

"Just give me a moment," he said, "I'll be right there. Can you leave the door ajar, please?"

"Okay," the old woman agreed, "Of course. But, first, I'll tell you a riddle. I haven't forgotten that nice one you told me about the leopard." She had a sly look on her face.

"It was a cheetah, not a leopard."

"Oh, that's right," she said. "I'm afraid my memory isn't what it used to be. Anyway, my riddle is, 'When is a door not a door?'"

Although Muffin knew the answer, he politely replied, "I don't know. When?"

"When it's a jar!" she shrieked and went back into her apartment. Muffin opened the suitcase and took something out.

Fox was already seated at the table in front of an empty plate. He had a big white napkin tucked under his chin and was holding a knife and fork and licking his lips. "Well," he said. "Was that who I think it was?"

The old woman winked. "He'll be right in."

At that moment, they heard the sound of steel scraping on the wood floor, and into the room rolled Muffin. He was inside a small cage on wheels. Pedaling up alongside the table, he did not get out of the cage.

With a smile, he said, "I'll have my tea in here, please." Fox stared at Muffin inside his cage.

"But why…" the old woman began.

"It makes me feel safer. If you knew how dangerous a muffin's life can be…" He turned to Fox. "I'm sure *you* know, sir, don't you?"

Fox, who had been studying the cage, did not answer. Instead, he suddenly leaned forward and reached through the narrow bars to try to unlatch the door.

"Uh-uh-uh-uh-uh!" cried Muffin, imitating Woody Woodpecker. He pressed a button, and the bars of the cage suddenly became molten red. A giant shock knocked Fox from his chair, unconscious, onto the floor. Calmly, Muffin unlatched the door of the cage, climbed up the leg of Fox's chair, and took his seat. Resting his feet on the fallen Fox, Muffin smiled at the old woman, who looked guilty and confused. "Milk and sugar, please."

## The End

FOR THOSE WHO complain about the predictable ruts into which families fall, consider this fictional memoir, prompted by a significant turnout of relatives at the launch of a chapbook I had written about my mother's family.[30] I probably should not have been surprised that so many of them turned up, but if I hadn't been, "Kith and Kindred" might not have been written.


## Kith and Kindred

### SNOS & KAHSLOP. J
### SREZITEPPA DNA STAEM ENIF FO SROYEVRUP


I KEPT NOTICING these faded letters on the dirty store window behind the heads of the last row of attendees. That is, I kept seeing something like them (since my laptop can't do mirror writing). They were the reverse of the sign I had seen when I arrived for my reading half an hour before:


### J. POLSHAK & SONS
### PURVEYORS OF FINE MEATS AND APPETIZERS


The reversed letters had an amusing resemblance to some obscure Slavic language, perhaps the one J. Polshak & Sons had spoken.

Are you surprised by the idea of a poetry reading in a defunct appetizing store? These days, many non-moneymaking events in our Brooklyn neighborhood take place at unorthodox venues: art

---

[30] "Jonathan Pintchik's" poems are from my collection, *Look to Mountains, Look to Sea* (River Otter Press, 2013)

shows in vacant retail spaces, drama and dance in defrocked churches and synagogues. "It's the economy, stupid!"

The reading was part of a series called Kith and Kindred: Partnering the Greats. So far, there had been three installments, two of which I had attended: *Where There's a Will: William Shakespeare and Willy Calhoun;* and *Meet the Miltons: John Milton and Milt Levitzsky.* There was also one I missed, *The Brooklynbury Tales,* which paired Chaucer with a Jeff—or a Jeremy—Something. Mine was the first one at the appetizing store, the others having occurred at a local library branch, which was reserved tonight for a bi-monthly contra-dance group.

My reading was called *Two Johns: John Keats and Jonathan Pintchik* (me). Although I had objected to the prostitution innuendo, the trio of young curators had overruled me, arguing that it would add a frisson. When twenty-five or thirty people showed up, mostly filling the three rows of folding chairs in front of the window, at first I thought the curators had been right. But the motivation for at least some in the audience turned out to be quite a different story.

Ten minutes after the announced starting time, curator Amy Stilton-Parks, a Goth, thanked everyone for coming, and read a boilerplate bio of Keats and a little puff about me. Moving front and center, I raised the mic and placed my manila folder on the lectern. Since I had been participating in readings for years, I was not too nervous, just a little pumped up. Thanking Ms. Stilton-Parks, and re-thanking the attendees, I launched into my intro:

"This series is based upon literary kinship. As tonight's title suggests, I claim kinship—affinity, at least—with John Keats, one of the great singing voices in the English language. Not to sound egotistical—even for a poet—(a titter), all I'm really claiming is that I write lyric poems—short, singing ones—with Keats as a model. I would like to…"

At this point, the voice of someone in the back whom I couldn't see—a piercing male tenor—interrupted. "Affinity!" cried the voice. "Yes, you both have two eyes, a nose, and a mouth—in your case, a big one." Since I had never been interrupted before—most crowds at readings are painfully polite—I was momentarily taken aback. The audience was, too. But then, a sixty-something woman with gray hair and black-rimmed glasses, seated in the center of the front row, loudly shh-ed the interrupter.

"That's okay, thanks," I said, and ventured a little pleasantry of my own. "I think the gentleman just wants me to shut up and read." Another titter.

I opened my folder to the four sheets I had prepared, each with a Keats poem on the left, and one of mine on the right. The plan was to alternate which poem I would read first, a tacit admission that comparisons would be invidious. But, just as I was about to start, something gave me pause: the identities of both interrupter and shh-er were coming into focus.

At my age—seventy-five—familiar faces and voices are tricky, especially at public events like readings. For various reasons, audience members tend to look and sound alike: friends, fellow writers, groupies, and just people who share the same gene pool.

I had decided to open with a tongue twister called "Fly, Firefly," because I knew that this poem, which I wrote in Maine decades ago, was an attention-getter. I would then segue into the Keats with an amusing anecdote. I began:

### Fly, Firefly

Insect inside:
deer fly died

fear fly fried.

Firefly, fire,
flare, firefly,
fair fly, fire…


Eureka: my own light went on! The interrupter was a hated
cousin on my father's side. Our last encounter had been in 1969
at a family party for the overflow from my wedding, where he
had insulted the bride while she was out of the room. I think the
insult was triggered by her scowl at one of his self-serving jokes.

"Congratulations, Jonathan," I think he had said, with a sour,
fat-faced grin, "I see your wife is passive-aggressive." As I
remember, I was too angry to reply. When I told Julie, she said
something un-passive, like "What a fucking asshole!" But don't
quote me, for, as she puts it, "You turn everything into a poem
or a story, dear."

By then, I had also placed the shh-er. She was Julie's first
cousin from Boston, who, over the years, had occasionally visited
us in Brooklyn. Leaving me at home, the two women would go
off to Manhattan together to look at art and eat lunch. I had last
seen this cousin, whose name eluded me, at Julie's funeral.

I cleared my throat and finished reading the tongue-twister,
stumbling once or twice:

…Flee, firefly,
fair fly, higher,
drear fleet fear.


Flee, fly, dear,
flee, fly, flow from

dire fly fighter.

Fie, fly frighter!

To forestall applause after every poem, I quickly launched into the anecdote. In case you don't know it, in December 1816, Keats—twenty-one—was visiting the eminent *literato*, Leigh Hunt. Since they were housebound by the weather, and getting bored, the jocular Hunt proposed a speedwriting contest. Inspired by a chirping cricket on the hearth, Keats had completed his minor masterpiece while the older poet was still licking his quill:


### On the Grasshopper and Cricket[31]

The Poetry of earth is never dead:
When all the birds are faint with the hot sun,
And hide in cooling trees, a voice will run
From hedge to hedge about the new-mown mead;
That is the Grasshopper's—he takes the lead
In summer luxury...

At this point, there was a second interruption, an excited, croaking, heavily accented woman's voice that seemed to come from the store window. "Yanu, Yanu!" it cried. "Summers, you

---

[31] John Keats, 'On the Grasshopper and Cricket," from *Selected Poems and Letters* (Boston, Houghton Mifflin, Riverside editions, 1952),19

used to spend with us. Remember, Yanu? Lots of crickets, lovely summers. In Jamesburg, on the farm."

My god. It was Minnie, my maternal grandmother, the one whose name for me was her approximation of "Jonathan." If that sounds strange, even stranger is the fact that Minnie died exactly half a century ago. The reason I remember is that her burial took place during the blizzard of 1966.

This time, no one shh-ed the interrupter, and I finished reading "On the Grasshopper and Cricket," meanwhile making eye contact with the audience—i.e. trying to spot my cousin and my grandmother.

 

…he has never done
With his delights; for when tired out with fun
He rests at ease beneath some pleasant weed.

The poetry of earth is ceasing never:
On a lone winter evening, when the frost
Has wrought a silence, from the stove there shrills
The Cricket's song, in warmth increasing ever,
And seems to one in drowsiness half lost,
The Grasshopper's among some grassy hills.

 

With a small bow, I invited the first, enthusiastic round of applause. (Did anyone even remember "Firefly?") As it died down, I said, "Don't you love that line, 'The poetry of earth is never dead?' Shall we move on?" The second pair would include one of my best.

But, before I could launch into "Ode to a Nightingale," there was—yes—a third interruption. This time, in a deep, also heavily accented—Middle European, I thought— voice, someone somewhere said, "That phrase you just used, Jonathan, 'move on,' is very evocative, very Keatsian. Yes, all things must move on, yourself included, both as an artist and as a man. Before it's too late."

In vain, I searched my memory banks. Based on the first two interrupters, I assumed this one must also be a relative. But all I could come up with was that he sounded like some shopkeeper- or craftsman-philosopher. Nineteenth Century? Early Twentieth? Could he have belonged to the paternal Hungarian branch, most of whom had been murdered by the Nazis shortly before my birth?

And so it went. Without describing the rest of the reading and interruptions, let me quote in its entirety the poem I paired with the "Nightingale" ode:

### Full Moon Reveals All

A full Moon lights the world tonight,
cutting a swath through reality.

Four plastic chairs bend in prayer
around a plastic table:
"Please, Moon, grant us sunsets,
so people come out and sit on us."
"Blessed are the cheap and uncomfortable,"
the understanding Moon intones,
"for they, too, shall be sat upon."

A yoke of lovers tiptoe down the road
from ticking car to sleeping house,
a pair of sneakers in one hand,

each other's, in the other.
They laugh because the road's so rough,
because the world is bright and clear,
because they have a secret.

Naughty Moon blankets Mother Cow
and, bending to a floppy ear,
whispers the lovers' secret.
Ear gives a twitch, but Cow sleeps on.
Can nothing lift this placid beast
from her complacency?

Having tired of chairs and cows
and of the needful human race,
Moon draws a cloud across her face
and turns to secrets of her own.

"Needful human race" indeed. If anything, after the first three interruptions, they became more and more needful. And, like *Star Wars* lasers, they seemed to shoot at me from all over the room, not just the store window, but above and below the audience, beneath my own feet, and through the ceiling right above my head. And every single interrupter was a relative, increasingly distant. Don't ask me how I knew that, I just did.

After the reading, too shaken to join Amy and the other curators for a beer, I went home, ate a snack, and retreated to bed. As you can imagine, my sleep that night was…interrupted. Most of the dreams featured the disembodied voices of relatives: "terrapin soup…" "slaving over a hot stove…" the candy store…" "says who?" "…stop by the office…"

But the worst dream of all came straight from the pages of history. This one flew me back a millennium, to a confrontation with the terrifying figure of Genghis Khan, no less, with whom, I read somewhere, millions of us share some of our DNA.[32] Brandishing a huge, curved sabre, and dressed in ornate silk robes and an iron and leather helmet, beneath which his long red hair hung down to his shoulders, The Great Khan fixed me with a blazing green eye,[33] and in a thick central-Asian accent, made an oracular pronouncement: "If you had not committed great sins, Jonathan, God would not have sent a punishment like me upon you." I think I read that he had actually said that to somebody (not me, of course).

The next morning, as I gulped my morning coffee and tried to sort through the welter of interruptions and dreams, I fixed upon the conqueror's pronouncement. In the clear light of day, instead of terrifying me, it made me furious. What nerve! I hope he comes back, so I can ask him exactly what my "great sins" were. I may also point out that I have never killed a single person, let alone forty million, like him.

Halfway into my second cup, I realized something else: most of my dreams, and most of the interruptions at the reading (Grandma's, excepted), had laid on pretty much the same guilt-trip that Genghis had, albeit less melodramatically. No wonder people hate their relatives.

In the week since the reading, I have done my best to put all that stuff behind me. But, so far, I have failed. Try as I may,

---

[32] Ewen Calloway, "Genghis Khan's Genetic Legacy has competition" Nature (23 January, 2015) www.nature.com/.../genghis-khan-s-genetic-legacy-has-competition-1.16.

[33] www.history.com/news/10-things-you-may-not-know-about-genghis-khan

whether I'm at my desk, out walking the dog—whatever—I can't stop seeing those letters on the window:

**SNOS & KAHSLOP. J**

Eighth or ninth cousins, no doubt, fourteen times removed.


**The End**

THIS NEXT MEMOIR, a fictionalized composite, combines the themes of families, books, and the past, which so often becomes the present, in the World of Gravy.


## IBS Rides the Internet

### February 28th, 2018:

IT HAS BEEN explained to me that even my title is open to confusion. My intention was to suggest an analogue to a story by my namesake, Isaac Bashevis Singer, which is about a misadventure from the days before cell phones (and the Internet). In "The Briefcase," the narrator is scheduled to give a lecture in Washington, D.C., but when he checks into his hotel, he discovers that he has brought the wrong briefcase from New York, not the one containing his notes. Frantic phone calls summon both his wife and "mistress" (pardon the anachronism), and a comic denouement ensues. I forget if he ever gets the notes.

Anyway, when I told Zoe, my daughter, the gist of my own misadventures, and mentioned my intended title, she informed me that "IBS" commonly stands for "Irritable Bowel Syndrome." Are acronyms taking over the world? Wondering what my own initials, "RTS," might stand for, I googled them, and found references ranging from several "Regional Transit Systems" to "*Radio Televizija Srbije*," or "Serbian Radio-Television."

Although I'm not a complete technophobe, I confess to an aversion to social media. The fact that I'm 76 may account for this aversion, but I do have my reasons. For example, I think social media are (is?) making people solipsistic and, in some ways, stupid, thereby exacerbating the global crisis of democracy. I only mention this aversion because it underlies the string of misadventures that comprise my narrative, which is now poised for lift-off, here at Cape Carnival.

* * *

THE TRIGGERING EVENT was a Facebook notification that arrived last Saturday evening. "They" said I had received a Google announcement from the wife of John Solomon, a former colleague. A legend in the classroom, John was also an old friend, and until his knees gave out, my favorite squash partner. When I last saw him a few months ago, he was slowly emerging from a supermarket, looking as if most of him was giving out. When I asked how he was, he told me he was suffering from heart disease and other unspecified ailments—unspecified, because he was still an ultra-Stoic.

As soon as I saw the notification, I said to Liz, my wife, "I think John may have died." She nodded, and returned to the *Times* crossword, which can be demanding on Saturday.

When I tried to open the announcement, Facebook led me through an unfamiliar process that I imagined would lead to John's wife's message. It didn't. Strangely, it led to a different message, which happened to be about the death of a different old man, Tim Parker, a friend from my Peace Corps days in Nigeria during the 1960s.

This message came from someone named "Robin Parker-Simmons," whom I guessed might be Tim's grandchild. Since I don't seem able to re-access the message now, I'll paraphrase it: There would be a funeral tomorrow, Sunday, for Timothy J. Parker, who died at age 78. The venue would be Thomas B. Goode & Sons, Funeral Home, on the Upper West Side of Manhattan. To facilitate further communications with the family, would I kindly provide Robin P.-S. with my e-mail address? I replied, indicating that I planned to attend, and providing the address. (Remember that.) Then, I pushed buttons and hoped for the best.

This last-minute funeral would require certain adjustments to my Sunday schedule. I had signed up for a midday squash round robin (another coincidence), which would have to be curtailed. Luckily, the courts were only a dozen short blocks from the funeral home. Liz and I had also been invited to our daughter, Zoe's, house in Brooklyn for Sunday dinner at six, but, unless the subways were even worse than usual, there should have been ample time for me to get there after the funeral.

Since I now had a big day ahead, I made myself get into bed early. But Tim's death caused a lot of vivid memories to bubble up. Possibly because they were at least half a century old, and I'm 3/4, they kept me from my beauty rest.

* * *

TO CALL TIM Parker a friend is a stretch. In the mid-1960s, most Peace Corps Volunteers (PCVs) in Africa were teachers, who worked at schools miles apart, and rarely saw each other. Although the Corps supplied us with Honda 50 motor scooters, some PCVs secretly purchased bigger machines. An engineering graduate of a midwestern university, Tim bombed around on a big Norton, sporting leather regalia, modified for the tropics. Our clique of scooter and motorcycle riders dubbed ourselves "The Ekiti Brothers," after the province where three of us worked. Although the other two, myself included, worked at schools in the contiguous Akoko province, "Ekiti Brothers" sounded better.

In a way, we were sort of a thinking man's Hell's Angels. Not that we were violent. I mean, Tim was a particularly gentle soul, and we were all in the *Peace* Corps, which most of us had joined to avoid the Vietnam War. But we would periodically meet, to bomb (and toot) around from bar to bar, stopping for beer, and trying to look impressive. Since irony was the name of the game, we laughed at our own act.

Once, in one of these roadside bars, the typical mud shack with corrugated tin roof, when the proprietor, a skinny, ragged young man, saw us, his eyes lit up. Before we could even order our drinks, he cried, "Ah, Americans! Yes. Let me show you something." And, leaving us to look at each other in amused surmise, he rushed to the back room.

A minute later, he returned with a 45 RPM record, which he carried with the utmost care, like a crown on a cushion. With equal care, he placed the record on a small plastic machine, and set it going. When we heard the scratchy lyrics, all five of us, including the Brother known for the least self-control, managed to limit our glee to broad smiles:

When it's pea-picking time in Georgia,
Apple-picking time in Tennessee,
Cotton-picking time in Alabama,
It's girl-picking time for me![34]

After expressing suitable appreciation, we ordered the usual: five local beers. "Warm," we specified, since, by then, we had all become acclimated. When the beer came, we settled into a desultory debate about the singer's identity. For some reason, we didn't ask to look at the label, and only years later did my musician son-in-law inform me that it was Jimmy Rodgers. He also corrected me: the first line was, "When it's *peach*-picking time in Georgia."

Recalling those days prompts both pride and mortification. The pride comes from my accomplishments as a PCV. For instance, I helped a colleague who had some construction experience lay out tennis and basketball courts at our school.

---

[34] www.lyricsmode.comJimmie Rodgers

Once, when we were trudging back from a stint at anchoring stanchions in concrete, we ran into a waggish Brit, who paraphrased Kipling: "Only mad dogs and PCVs go out in the midday sun." Since then, whenever I see a Nigerian in the NBA, I enjoy a moment of pride—unearned, since, as far as I know, no basketball pro ever attended that school.

✳ ✳ ✳

ASSOCIATIONAL THINKING APPLIES not only to dreams, but to night thoughts. In this case, the "court" theme brought me back to John Solomon, my still-living ex-squash partner. John introduced me to the sport during the summer of 1979, when we both happened to be in Oxford, England. In his delightful, peremptory manner, he suggested we meet early the next morning, and that I bring along my sports "kit." When we met, he silently led me past the house of the Master of the College where he was an alumnus, and through the gardens to a building that looked like a big shed. Stepping over a high threshold, he flipped a switch, and I found myself in a big boxlike structure with white walls and red lines.

"Here," he said, extracting a racquet from his own kit. "Let's get started." Thus began thirty-nine delightful years, and counting, of squash.

✳ ✳ ✳

BACK TO NIGERIA, 1965 or 1966…an even more laudable project than the courts, I think, was helping to raise money for a social club, where the elite from the town's multiple ethnicities (Yoruba, Edo, Ibo, Hausa-Fulani) could amicably drink and play darts or ping pong. Of course, this feeling of accomplishment has been marred by the fact that my tenure witnessed the ethnically fueled political crisis that led to the horrific Biafra War.

165

As for the *Easy Rider* act of The Ekiti Brothers, it was innocuous enough, I suppose, although we certainly made fools of ourselves. Assuming they even cared, I blush to imagine what our female counterparts said about us (even though Tim was a heartthrob.) Still, if we did any real damage, it was probably to the already war-tarnished reputation of the United States.

Perhaps our most outstanding folly was an eight-millimeter home movie that we made over the course of about a year. Although this movie was supposed to be a sort of lampoon of the real *Easy Rider*, it was closer to *The Keystone Cops in Africa*. The main action had us riding around the countryside, stopping to whoop it up at bars, like the one where we heard the song. Instead of provoking violence from local bigots, however, our antics provoked unfeigned hilarity in the delighted onlookers, and also contributed to the local economy.

The film's plot, such as it was, conflated the resource-looting theme of *Heart of Darkness* with the work of Dr. Albert Schweitzer. A main prop was a big piece of wood, painted white to resemble, faintly, an elephant's tusk. Wearing a pith element, a long-sleeved safari shirt, and baggy pants belted at the chest, my character was "Dr. Cyril Schmutzer." In several scenes, I tried to lobotomize one of The Brothers, on the theory that this would turn him into a virtuous Christian. When I finally succeeded, the guy who played my victim, a recently deceased, non-observant Jew, made a very funny tropical zombie. We called this concoction *The Lesson*, because we framed it as a blackboard lecture on morality by Dr. Schmutzer. Tim, the gentlest, kindest Brother, played a feral gang member.

I forget how the movie ended, but I do remember what happened to the only copy. After his Peace Corps days, the guy who shot it (who went on to become a documentarian of minor note) moved to Roxbury, in Boston. When his apartment was robbed, he spent days and nights searching through dumpsters and garbage cans, and posting reward notices, all to no avail. Oh, well, *ars longa.*

❋ ❋ ❋

AT SOME POINT, my night thoughts segued into memories from family history, on my father's side. Like the Peace Corps memories, many of these were ludicrous. A notable one was the funeral of my aunt Rachel. In the course of repeating it over the years, I may well have mythologized this event. Since, for some reason, I attended it alone, and since I have lost touch with that side of the family, there were no witnesses. As Liz, an artist herself, once remarked after listening to another supposedly true story, "You're a writer, dear. You make things up."

Aunt Rachel had been a committed member of the Workmen's Circle, a progressive, pro-labor group that still exists. I remember the funeral as a duet. The first voice was that of the presiding official, a sort of secular cleric. A very short man with a small mustache and an extremely nasal voice, his eulogy was based on the cliché that life is like a book. The line I remember is, "If some of us leave behind large, even massive tomes, full of adventures and accomplishments, Rachel's book is a slim volume containing but a single theme, her beloved family."

I think I must have been in college at the time, and both of Rachel's sons were already grown men. I remember them as a pair of big, round heads in the front row of the room in which the service took place. At this point in their lives, both were fat, like most of my dad's family.

While I was trying not to laugh at the ridiculous eulogy, I was also regaled with a private lecture. This was a shouted whisper in my ear by an uncle-by-marriage sitting behind me. Family legend had it that this man, a large, stooped, beetle-browed German-Jew who married into our Ashkenazi family, was a dull-witted lawyer whose practice depended on the Albany

167

connections of his clever wife, another aunt, who was either a secretary to powerful politicians, or scrubbed their floors.

"Ronny," the lawyer kept saying, in a deep, loud whisper, with his strong accent, "why don't you ever visit me at the office? Come up some time. I'll show you around, take you out for a nice lunch…"

He repeated this invitation, or plea, several times, only shutting up when Rachel's sons simultaneously swiveled their heads and made exaggerated shushing gestures. I remember tears running down their faces, which I suppose were prompted not by indignation over the loud whispering, or by the eulogy, but by their mother's death.

At around two a.m., I mentally strolled through the paternal portrait gallery. It was quite a collection. Among my uncles were a hard-drinking longshoreman who lost a leg to diabetes (they all had this condition), and who was married to a jolly, forbearing Polish woman who looked like a polar bear; and the eldest brother—still alive by the time I came along—a cab driver and bookie, bald, saggy and fish-faced. When my dad would take me to see the Knicks or fake wrestling at the old Madison Square Garden, I remember this uncle leaning against his cab door, near the 50th Street entrance, counting money and chewing on the stub of a disgusting cigar. His wife, as I recall, managed a department store cafeteria, Macy's or Gimbels.

My dad's sisters were also what were then called "characters." In addition to the two already mentioned, there was a zany former ballerina married to a Hungarian anarchist, whose "day job" was as a fur cutter. Since fur-cutting was a seasonal, piece work occupation, this sallow, seedy uncle-by-marriage seldom seemed to be employed, leading to my industrious father's jokes, such as that his brother-in-law never went out on a job in winter—too cold—or summer—too hot—or autumn—a leaf might fall on his head. (What about spring?) The name of this uncle-by-marriage was "Manny," which prompted my dad to refer to him as "Manual Labor." I think I inherited the paternal gene for waggishness.

* * *

AT ANY RATE, by the time I dragged myself out of bed that Sunday morning, my main worry—selfish, as usual—was how I would manage to get through the round robin without injury. (The motto of aging squash players is, "Live to play another day.") As I often do nowadays, I ate a filling breakfast replete with sugar and carbs to compensate for insufficient sleep.

In any event, the squash session, though truncated, went fine. During a break, when I told my partners where I was going afterwards, and mentioned the odd pathway by which the invitation had arrived, one of the younger players explained that this was how the Facebook messaging service worked. He said that he had once had a similar experience, when he tried to open one message, and found another one.

Reassured, I finished playing, showered, dressed, and started for the funeral home. As it happened, I had allowed so much time that I wound up with fifteen minutes to kill, which I did at a pocket park three blocks from my destination. Since the day was sunny and warm for February, this interlude was no hardship. What I remember about the park was how interesting everything looked. You would think I had never seen a poodle or a baby carriage before. I was on high alert.

At five minutes to two, half-a-block from Thomas B. Goode & Sons, I started searching for familiar faces. I saw only one, a medium-sized old boy wearing the costume of an academic: tweed jacket, glasses, and a woolen tie. (I was wearing a dark shirt and pants and my everyday black winter coat, but no jacket or tie.) Although we were heading in the same direction, the man did not look like an Ekiti Brother, or, for that matter, anyone else

169

I had ever known. Nor did he acknowledge me. Of course, we might both have changed beyond recognition.

As I walked through the main entrance of the funeral home, the uniformed doorman did not ask me to open my backpack. This was a surprise, since you might think that, these days, funeral homes were inviting targets for terrorism. The shabby vestibule, and the receptionist, who sat at a table perpendicular to the entrance, carried me back to funerals of the past, including Aunt Rachel's. Everything—the lighting, furniture, even the carpet—wore the muted tones of solemnity.

Since I had no idea what had become of Tim Parker over the years, I anticipated that, for me, the eulogy might be what is sometimes called "a learning experience." But, maybe, one of The Ekiti Brothers who had kept in touch would say a few—or a few thousand—words about those disgraceful old days.

"Can I help you?" asked the receptionist, a heavyset man of a certain age. Even his smile seemed muted, a hedge against the presumed grief of his interlocutors. When I approached the table, he did not stand up.

"Yes, thanks," I replied. "I'm looking for a 'Timothy Parker,' please. I'm an old friend."

The man looked baffled. Checking his handwritten list of the day's funerals, which was very short, he shrugged. "I'm afraid I don't see that name. We do have a service at two, but the deceased is…" and he gave a different name. "Are you sure you're in the right place?" He mentioned a nearby, rival funeral parlor.

"Huh," I said. Extricating my old-fashioned print datebook from my backpack, I showed him the name and address of his own establishment, which made him raise his eyebrows, and think for a moment.

"You know," he said, "our two o'clock is on the fourth floor. Why not go up and see if you recognize anyone?"

"But why…?"

He shrugged. "Stranger things happen. People change their names, and so on. It will only take you a minute." And he pointed toward an elevator at the rear of the lobby. Mostly from curiosity, I walked across, and pushed the button. Running the elevator when it arrived was a young man, also in a dark suit, who seemed to be playing a card game on his smart phone during our slow ride.

When we reached four, I found myself in a generic, old-fashioned chapel, with pews, a guestbook, and some religious paraphernalia. Although, by now, it was a few minutes after two, people were still milling around, greeting each other, signing a guestbook, and beginning to get settled. Their faces wore the usual range of funeral expressions, from solemn (the majority), to determinedly cheerful (some), to devastated (a few). I did spot the tweedy professor, and a round-faced young fellow of about twenty, who looked familiar. But neither they nor anyone else looked anything like Tim or the three other Brothers who, as far as I knew, were still extant, and whom I thought I might have recognized in their current incarnations. Obviously, I was at the wrong funeral.

After a minute or two of wandering around staring at people, I noticed a big bouncer-like guy giving me the eye. So I threaded my way against traffic and took the elevator back down to the lobby. Still at his table, the receptionist beckoned me over.

"Sorry," he said. "I checked our database." With a shrug, he gestured behind himself to a desktop computer that I could see through the open door of an office. "No record of any funeral for a 'Timothy Parker' during the last six months." I thanked him and left.

Back on the street, I felt at loose ends. I was not due at my daughter's house for three hours, and she had told me she was working a co-op shift this afternoon, and her husband was taking my grandson to a Pokémon tournament, or something. Walking toward the subway entrance on Central Park West, I cut through the small park that abuts the back entrance to the Hayden Planetarium, which, in turn, abuts the Museum of Natural History.

What could have happened? When in doubt, I call Liz, my go-to confidante. As I was thinking of doing this, I remembered that one of Rachel's sons used to live in the fancy apartment building on 81st Street across from which I was standing. Having long disliked this cousin, I found myself replaying a snippet from an encounter at a family event.

"How're you doing these days?" I had asked.

"Not too well. I hate the human race."

"Everyone?"

"Pretty much."

What could you say to that?

Those were my thoughts as I strolled through the small park. Then, I called Liz at her studio. When I told her about the non-funeral, she was as puzzled as I was.

"I'm right behind the Planetarium," I said. "Since I have three hours to kill, I think I'll walk across Central Park to the library." I was referring to a private library we belong to on East 79th Street. "It's such a nice day."

"Good idea." She thought for a moment. "Wait a minute. Didn't your friend Tim die a while ago? Am I crazy? I think we were on vacation somewhere, and I sort of remember reading about it in the paper."

"Huh. Now that you mention it, I vaguely remember the same thing. Or was that a different Peace Corps friend?"

"No, I think it was Tim."

When we had repeated our plan to meet at Zoe's house and disconnected, I decided I was too tired even to walk to the library. I would just take the subway home. If the train gods were smiling,

I could drop off my squash kit, have a nap, and still get to Brooklyn on time.

This plan worked. At five forty-eight, I was walking up the hill from the subway, when who should I see coming down the hill, but Liz? The fact that we met right in front of Zoe's house—Liz had taken a bus from the studio—seemed like an uptick in fortune. We hugged, rang the bell, and went inside to a cheerful dinner. One highlight was the sense that our nine-year-old grandson—who ate everything, laughed at all my jokes, and joined in the conversation—was "developing beautifully." A large part of the dinner conversation, of course, focused on my Internet misadventure, and Liz repeated her hunch that Tim had died previously.

As I said, this pleasant dinner, and the swift resolution of my confusion, confirmed my sense of a turn in fortune. The resolution was my son-in-law's doing. After listening patiently to my account of the mix-up, he easily cleared it up, elaborating on what my squash partner had said.

"Liz may be right," he explained. "When Google messages accumulate, and you try to check one, they sometimes key you into an old one. I'm not sure why this happens. I bet if you searched your friend on the 'Net, you'd find out he died a while ago." To his credit, my son-in-law did not show a trace of the condescension that I, an ignorant old fool, deserved. Such a simple explanation for such an apparently complicated string of errors.

He was right. When I got home, a search readily yielded a paid death notice for "Parker, Timothy J." that had appeared in *The Times* about a year before. Included among the relatives of the beloved deceased was a grandson, Robin Parker-Simmons.

∗ ∗ ∗

THAT MIGHT HAVE ended the IBS saga, but—surprise—it didn't. This morning, six days after the non-event, I received an email from Robin. It occurred to me that this might be a response to my belated acknowledgment of the funeral invitation, in which, you may remember, I had provided contact information.

The first part of the email was sweet. Tim had often reminisced about me and the other "Efiti" Brothers. (A Freudian typo?) He had mentioned what a smart, funny guy I was. Then came the kicker:

The other day, Mr. Singer, I gave your contact info to the other surviving member of the gang, Peabody Farnsworth, whom I met at my granddad's funeral. Mr. Farnsworth emailed me, and said he wanted to get back in touch with you. My bad, for not asking your permission first."

Oh, no—after half a century. Pea Farnsworth, the butt of all our jokes, and, if I say so, myself, a ridiculous buffoon. During one drunken episode, this sloppy prep-school groupie had belched and farted simultaneously, prompting Tim to quip, "Shot out in front, and blown out behind." We must have repeated this witticism a hundred times.

A second anecdote about Pea involved oatmeal cookies (or were they chocolate-chip?). Misreading a recipe, the houseboy of the colleague who made the "mad dogs and PCVs" wisecrack had taken the abbreviation for tablespoons (tbsp.) of baking powder for teaspoons (tsp). Soon after the cookies had been served—and the mistake, discovered—Pea came putting along on his Honda 50. Joining us in the Brit's sitting room, he scarfed down six or eight of the soapy cookies. While we all struggled to keep from pissing ourselves, oblivious to the fact that no one else was eating any, Pea kept saying how good they were. His favorite adjective was "keen."

Extrapolating, I'd guess that, by now, Peabody Farnsworth, Esq. was a retired, thrice-divorced insurance executive, who maxed out his credit card every month, and suffered from obesity and related ailments. But I didn't have to guess. Scrolling through the rest of my emails, I found one from peafarn@gmail.com. Before I opened it, I guessed what it said:

"Yo, Ron Singer, how're they hanging, bro? After all these years! Remember me, Old Pea Farnsworth? Since Tim, Jerry, and Ben have all bought the farm by now—sad, very sad—you and I should get together *pronto* (while we still can). From time to time, I train down to the Big Apple from this dull CT 'burb, so what say we knock back a few brews and swap some lies about the old days? Remember *The Lesson*, bro, in which you starred as that brilliant savant, Dr. Schnitzer?"

Aside from three minor details, my guess was right: Pea lived not in Connecticut, but Westchester; instead of "a few brews," he suggested dinner at an expensive restaurant; and he referred to me, correctly, as "Dr. Schmutzer."


Thus are we all dogged, for better, and for worse, by the mistakes of the past.


**The End**

RETURNING TO MY wife, Liz's, side of our family, I wrote this elegy, of sorts, after the death of her father, Sam Yamin, the widowed husband of Elsie Yamin (quoted in the epigraph to this book):

## My Father-in-Law, Eighty-Eight
## (as he enters his apartment building)

To die is to leave this beautiful city,
city of color and light:
the blue-black sky, dusk of early Summer,
day going grandly into night,
and the clear, cutting light
of fine days in Autumn and Spring,
the light that gives the buildings
their full dimensionality.

Coming home from a walk in the park,
blue-black sky, the very edge of dark,
newspaper tucked beneath my arm,
I tip my hat to a neighbor,
a very old widow with a very small dog.
Ritual politesse, abiding civility.

Then I turn for a last look at the plane trees
standing in a crooked line across the street,
their new little leaves silhouetted
against the richly shadowed pink stone
of the wide solid buildings.

Every day now, every day,
these things I stop to see and feel
once more—and, oh, once again—
before I come up to this empty…


And here, at last, is my full-blown fictional memoir about my mother's family, which I hope I have not foreshadowed to death.

## RANU M'ZOOKA
## SUMMARY

THE FAMILY SAGA runs from the escape of the sisters' parents, Sam and Bessie Kaufman (née Aronoff), from Russia during the first decade of the Twentieth Century, to Betty and Estelle's deaths about a century later. In between, the first children were born on Delancey Street, in Manhattan; the next ones, including Betty, on Boerum Street, Brooklyn; and the final batch, including Estelle, in New Jersey. Like all of their siblings, Betty and Estelle would move back to New York City, and like several of the others, they would end up in Florida. The Epilogue to Parts One and Two, by my daughter, Zoe Singer, carries the story into a fourth generation.

In all, there were six surviving children. Betty was the third-born and Estelle the fifth. The others were Harry (#1), Jean (#2), Jack (#4), and Sandy (#6). Jack lived into his nineties, and Jean, into her late eighties, but the lives of Harry and Sandy were sadly truncated.

*A Voice for My Grandmother* is based on family legends, (inaccurate) memories, and my imagination. Most of the material for *Betty and Estelle* comes from a ninety-eight-minute interview conducted on June 14th, 1997 with my mother, Betty Singer

(November 24th, 1911 – August 21st, 1997), and her sister, Estelle Spelke (November 29th, 1916 – November 21st, 2002). The interview took place at Estelle's apartment in Tamarac, Florida, about a mile from my mother's apartment. The interviewers were Estelle's second child, Michele Spelke, and Michele's late husband, Bob Yuell.

Then, on December 1st, 2001, Michele and her brother, Ken Spelke, conducted a second interview as they drove Estelle around the family's principal home town, Jamesburg, New Jersey, which is about twenty miles from the nearest large town, New Brunswick. Much of this interview took the form of "Oh, look. That's where…"

By 1997, both sisters were widows. Five months after the 1997 interview, my mother died, and five years after that, less than a year after the second interview, so did Estelle. Thus, both sisters lived to be eighty-six, in a sense completing a cycle of close affinity. Surviving today are Estelle's three children, Karen, Michele, and Ken. The four of us are now among the old people in our family.

"Grandpa Sets the Record Straight" is a fantasy in which I try to pull the first two parts together.

# 1. A VOICE FOR MY GRANDMOTHER

## I. LATER YEARS

### Snapshots

SHE SITS AT a table by a window, her mouth, with its two teeth, working, her hands playing with knots in a hanky.

The window is in a generic, not a specific, apartment, but it's a kitchen window—her sphere.

The weather, too, is unspecific: it could be rain, sun, snow.

"Zu hot," she says, but that could be the steam.

Can she read? Why doesn't she talk more? Probably the language.

She smells of two kinds of powder, face and bubblegum.

She eats corn on the cob by cutting and scraping all the kernels off, then eating them one by one. It takes a long time. But so what?

She looks like an imaginary old Indian chief, referred to by my dad and me, but not by her daughter, my mom, as "Ikamatubee." Or was there really some notable chieftain of that name?

### The Shoes

WHENEVER SHE THOUGHT about the shoes, which was once every few years, her third, and youngest, daughter would become incensed.

"When Mom needed a new pair of shoes, Pop wouldn't even take her into the city to buy them. He'd wrap up the old ones in newspaper and ride the train in, himself, then go down to the lower East Side and buy exactly the same shoes—same style, same color, same size."

Imagine: Grandma's shoes becoming a talking point in a debate about sexism!

"I can think of a million things that story leaves out."

"Like what? Like what color were the shoes? And what did she wear while he was gone?"

We're probably supposed to picture her traipsing around the farm barefoot.

Maybe she hated going into the city.

Maybe those were the shoes she liked.

Maybe.


## Two Wicked Sons-in-Law

MY FATHER MADE mother-in-law jokes about Grandma that I can't remember. He hated religion, but, while my mother was getting out the kosher dishes—preparatory to a visit—he would raise the banner of tolerance, proudly proclaiming a moratorium on anti-religious jokes.

He would also ask my mom how long Grandma was going to stay, then rip into his favorite topic, inequity, in this case the alleged fact that the other relatives didn't shoulder their fair share of Grandma time.

Although she still kept her small apartment, she really couldn't live alone any longer. The money contributed by each of her five then-living children made for a second inequity complaint. Money was a vexed topic; very.

The math of each of these two inequities was inscrutable, always open to profound debate. Dad would also complain about inequity on a global scale—racial, economic, and so on—and he would use the same tone as when he complained that last year this or that relative had only let Grandma stay at their house half as long as she had stayed at ours. The alleged chief culprit was my uncle, the husband of the daughter who told the shoe story. Social justice may have suffered from being made to share the stage with petty complaint.

Nor was decorum a cherished value. When they thought it was time for Grandma to leave, both my father and uncle would make jocular throat-clearing noises, then drop rude, obvious hints. My uncle even did this in front of me once. Har, har! The latitude of these scenes was about two degrees south of a sitcom. The boorish sons-in-law did, however, like Grandma's cooking. Is there no one to forgive these men?


## Ranu, M'zooka

"RANU, M'ZOOKA," she would say, as she came through the door.

She would rummage through her huge patent-leather pocketbook and bring out a very large packet of bubblegum: Bazooka, a segmented log, pink and speckled with sugar. One by one, I would stuff as many segments as I could into my mouth— four? five?—and, when the bubble broke, it would cover my whole face.

"Ranu!" she would laugh, trying to look strict.

I was eight or nine in this memory. Was that Swahili she was speaking? Was the gift made from love or from a desire for acceptance? Who can possibly say? Grandma, like my own mom, lived in loving fear.

"Pocketbook, money, keys." According to my mother that was my first utterance. Improbable.

Grandma never had a word to throw at a dog. She'd sit there smiling and nodding, and, once in a while, reach over and pat my hand.

"There was something, like, very, like, Sixties about Granny. Like, good vibes, man. Like."

"Roll me a J, Gran?"

"No, Ranu. M'zooka."


## Grandma's Bones

RECENTLY, A SCANDAL broke. The funeral company that buried Grandma twenty years ago, a large, respected old concern, was discovered to have overbooked. Gravestones had disappeared. Split-level burials were unearthed; Mausoleums had been sledge-hammered to make room for multiple newcomers. Bones were found dumped in the adjacent woods.

Is Grandma now in the woods? What happens to corpses matters a lot to Jews—religious ones, that is. My dad and my uncle would first have waxed indignant over the scandal, and then, although the latter was, himself, observant, made numerous self-convulsing jokes.

"Ranu. Over here. Under that big bush, M'zooka."


## Another Grandma: The Council Person

"ARE YOU KIDDING?" cried the feisty septuagenarian grandma. "You can't give out a twenty-million-dollar contract without any bids. Not even in this town. And, if you try to railroad it through, so help me, I'll go to the papers. The taxpayers didn't elect me to let people like you rob them."

A woman like my Grandma, in many ways: old, similar origins, even looked a bit like her. But the councilperson had not been married to someone who was said to have bought her shoes for her. And before that? In their earlier lives? There must have been other cardinal differences. Possibly, though, somewhere inside her, Grandma had the same spirit—somewhere.

## Sentimental Depictions of the Aged

THERE ARE FEW things I hate more than stories about lonely, impoverished oldsters sitting by their windows feeling bored and bereft. I don't even like these characters when they turn up in English murder novels as the neighborly snoops who peep through the curtains for twenty years until, one fatal day, they see something which solves the whole case. They, and the writers, for that matter, should get a life. Anyway, they, the writers, need better plots.

## A Turn of Phrase

HER SECOND DAUGHTER, my mother, inherited a turn of phrase, which she began to draw upon in middle age:

"How are you, Mom?"

"Oh, about the same."

Not "Good." Never, "I'm well." Not even, "Fine, thanks."


## II. EARLIER YEARS

## The Domestic Economy: Eggs

GRANDPA, A FAILED chicken farmer, morphed into something like a gentlemen farmer.

Verily, it was chicken shit which broke most of the mighty men of old, from the pale, scrawny scholars to the giants on the Earth. Getting rid of the constant, copious droppings before they turned to cement must have been like cleansing the Augean Stables. Among the Jewish-American diaspora, failure at chicken farming was practically a tradition.

So Grandpa became an entrepreneur, buying wholesale from those martyrs and supermen who stayed the course, and transporting product to the nearest large town, where he would retail it door to door. Did he travel by horse and wagon at first? Grandma's help would have been essential: he did the money and eggs, she did the rest—the home fires, and all that.

Some protein-poor people are superstitious about eggs. For instance, the Yoruba of the tsetse-ridden West African rainforest have a proverb, "The child who is given eggs to eat will grow up to be a thief." Unfortunately, we lack statistics.

## And a Mimetic Micro-Economy

I, MYSELF, PLAYED Store with the little granddaughter, my age, from across the road. (Was Doctor also played? Quite possibly.) Pebbles, sticks, grapes, flowers, and pinecones and needles were purveyed across a marble counter in our sun-dappled arbor. She bought, I sold.

At least once, Grandma must have walked up the hill to look on in approval, nodding, smiling, and wiping her hands on her apron.

## Personal Cows

THERE WAS A cow for each of the gentleman farmer's five children, all with predictable names—"Bossy," "Spotty," and so forth. Although each child was expected to care for their own cow, the ultimate responsibility for all five of these charismatic mega-faunae must have fallen to Grandma. Not to mention the responsibility for all five children.

Or were there six, or even seven, of each? One or two children may already have died or gone their ways by the time my generation came along. If so, what happened to their personal cows, not to mention the five others? Don't ask.

# Fidei Defensor

OTHERS AMONG THE Jews in the area made more money. The big thriving farm down the road where my cousins, friends, and I pretended to be robbers as we helped ourselves to fallen apples and pears has long since been transformed. Although the dairy still supplies milk to the environs and beyond, the rest of the farm has been carved into a spiffy but dull housing subdivision and a big ugly office block, the centerpiece of the whole agglomeration. Each of these enterprises bears the name of the original farm from which we children once gleaned.

It was my own Grandpa, however, a man of only middling wealth, who took the lead in matters spiritual. Rabbis were brought over from Russia. They lived in our house, at least initially, and we hosted services for the synagogue-less little community. When one of these men moved on, whether upward or downward, money had to be found by means of which to extract, lure, and ferry over the next one.

Bickering must have been inevitable. The family was large, and Grandpa brought these strangers into the space which Grandma, in a sense, ruled, inviting their empty stomachs to her table. But since she remained observant years later, long after Grandpa had left the scene, she presumably concurred with his acts of pious charity. Without him, no religious life for the Jewish families in this, their new land. And so, presumably, none without her.

## Grandpa Dies

THIS TIME, WE stayed longer, on into the fall, to help see Grandpa through his end game. School, regrettably, was missed. He had inoperable, excruciating cancer somewhere in the nether regions. He screamed and screamed, then screamed some more.

"Why didn't they give him morphine or something?"

a. "They did, but after a while it stopped working."

b. "They couldn't give him enough. It was expensive."

This was a horrible time for everyone. My cousins and I were old enough to be almost told he was dying. Whichever daughters were then in residence saw him through the nights in shifts, and their exertions heaped unwonted burdens of parenting and emotional support on their own overtaxed husbands.

But it was Grandma who must have borne the brunt both of Grandpa's care and of the household regimen, which, as always, had to be kept up.

And what happened to all the eggs?


## A Note in the Interest of Equity

I CANNOT REMEMBER anyone ever having suggested that our long sojourns at my grandparents' house be credited against the account of Grandma's subsequent visits to us. The bottom line would have been, to use one of my mom's favorite adjectives, interesting.

But never mind. By now, I am the family's principal surviving earthly accountant.


## Leisure Time

WHEN MY MOTHER was growing up, baseball was played in a big field on the property. My mother's younger brother, a real athlete, "made the girls play in the outfield, way back in the outfield."

In my time, we would swim and picnic in the park at the top of the dam on the small lake in the middle of town. Grandma and Grandpa were never there. They must have been working, or relaxing at home, whatever form that would have taken:

a. read the paper and/or religious texts

b. sewed, knitted, crocheted

c. listened to the radio

d. sat on the porch, rocking and praying for a breeze

e. some, all, or none of the above

f. and, oh yes, once all the children were in place, any bedroom activity becomes a matter of (im)pure speculation.

Or, maybe, they just sat staring into space. Or dozed. They probably dozed.

# 2. BETTY AND ESTELLE

## New Brunswick

AFTER THE FIRST Jamesburg years, the family moved to New Brunswick, where they lived next to the Raritan River.

**Betty:** We used to walk up and down the street with the neighbors upstairs. I made a few friends; it was like living. On the farm, there was nothing.

(In front of the building, Sam operated a small luncheonette, where he sold sandwiches to the workers from the wholesale market across the road. By then, my mother was in third grade. Almost eighty years later, still sheepish, she made a confession. Explaining that her father never remembered to give her milk money for school, she would just take "some change" from the "little thing" where he kept the money from the sandwiches. "That was when I did a little stealing.")

## The Big House

**BETTY:** THE DOCTORS told my parents that Sandy had a condition. He'd be better off living in a more countrified atmosphere. He was coughing, or something.

**Estelle:** So whatever…we moved [back] to Jamesburg. First of all, we were a big family in a small apartment, in New Brunswick.

"Condition," "Countrified": two staples of my mother's euphemistic lexicon. At any rate, the family moved into a large home beside the railroad tracks on Gatzmer Avenue, which they were soon calling The Big House. This house still stands.

**Estelle:** It was all the way across town from school. We walked all the way to school every day, in all kinds of weather, a whole bunch of us. Nobody picked me up, and nobody drove me…The Big House. It sounds like a reformatory.

**Betty:** No! When it was sold, it became an old age home…there were five upstairs bedrooms and four downstairs rooms, including the library. And that's where we had our services. Keeping the house warm was a big problem. You couldn't play the piano, because your hands would freeze. Later [when Estelle was a teenager], Sam put in a bathroom and central heating.

**Estelle:** Betty jumped ahead. This was still the time of the outhouse. You know how President Carter's mother got on top of [sic] the television one time and said they were very comfortable, because they had a three-holer? [My mother titters.] Well, our family only had a one-holer, so we must have been rather poor…

(The sisters agreed that the house always had running water, but only in the kitchen, where they bathed in a galvanized tub with water heated in the stove. They disagreed about whether they got dressed under the feather beds upstairs or in front of the stove.)

**Estelle:** I can describe my little room almost like Picasso described his little house with the chestnut tree outside.

**Betty:** The three brothers shared the first big bedroom. Remember, Estelle?

**Estelle:** Yes. I don't know why. Jean had a room, and you had a room. And I had a little room.

**Betty:** Then, you shared a room with me. We had a double bed. We wanted to sleep together because it was warmer. We used to talk half the night. We were always close, from then on.

# The Train

**ESTELLE:** WHEN WE first moved in, I was out in the yard right beside the railroad tracks. I saw the train coming, and, you know, when you see a train coming in the distance…it looked like it was coming straight at me. And I ran into the house, frantic. I said, "This train is coming into our house!" [The sisters laugh.] I must have been five years old. My mother would say, "No, it's going to stay on the track."

## "That's Unusual. Isn't It?"

WHEN THEY FIRST moved into the big house, they heard peeping from upstairs and discovered that, for the sake of warmth, chicks had been hatched in the top dresser drawer in a closet in one of the bedrooms.

**Betty:** That's unusual, isn't it?

**Estelle (roaring with laughter):** I would hope so!

## Housekeeping

**BETTY:** JEAN…USED to boss me around. And I wouldn't boss anyone around.

**Estelle (laughing):** That's not unusual for the older child. She was busy. She was babysitting, and she did cooking.

## A BRIEF LIFE OF JEAN: THE ELDEST DAUGHTER

JEAN NEVER PUT hardship behind her. After an arranged marriage to a man who turned out to be an alcoholic, she became a practical nurse. Widowed early, and always poor, she raised two daughters as best she could. Later in life, Jack bought an apartment for his big sister in Palm Beach, Florida, the town to which his wife's wealthy parents had already retired.

Whenever we drove up from Tamarac to visit her, Jean's loving heart would swell, and she would cook for us the same traditional foods her mother used to cook. As soon as my father saw the steaming Jewish-style chicken stew with potatoes, carrots, and raisins, and the baked noodle pudding (also with raisins) emerge from the kitchen, his little-boy eyes would grow huge, and he would dig right in. I think my Auntie Jean had the sweetest smile of anyone I have ever known.

## Holidays

IF, AS IS often said, God is in the details, many of the details in the Kaufman household were theocentric.

**Estelle**: My mother had this huge kitchen. On the holidays, all the services were in our house, it was called a *schul* [synagogue], and they all came. We had a long table, and that table, after services, was filled with all kinds of Jewish goodies—pickled herring, baked challah—and she used to prepare all of that. An *Oneg Shabbat*, they call it today. And the kids were off from school, so they would come, too. And, while the parents were praying, we would have a ball playing with each other. It was such a good childhood. And that's where we developed these very strong friendships. When I get together with my friend, Ruth Goldstein, who's now Ruth Wertheimer, nobody in the world exists except us. And the games. We invented games that nobody ever heard of. It would be dark upstairs, and half of us would be separated into those that hid, in the closets, under the beds, and half...

**Betty**: Hide and Seek.

**Estelle** (laughing): And those of us who were...the ones who seek...would make up the craziest, zaniest stories, expressions, to get them to laugh. And, if they laughed, we'd find them.

# The Family Photograph

**BETTY**: YOU KNOW that family picture we have? He put us all in the truck one Saturday and took us to the photographer.

**Estelle**: It's a lovely picture. I was about seven.

**Betty**: I was about twelve.

**Estelle**: I remember they wanted to put me further back, and I argued with the photographer, "No, no, my new shoes won't show." How funny it is, the things you can remember from years ago.

**Betty**: It's interesting.

**Estelle**: My father sat, and my mother stood. Is that still the case with photography?

## AFTER THE BIG HOUSE

AFTER THE BIG house, the family lived for about four years in "the little house" on nearby Possum Hollow Road, where Sam added two extra rooms. There was a stuffed owl on the fireplace in the living room of this house. Many years later, my parents' living room in their retirement condominium featured ceramic owls (as well as ceramic turtles).

Many of my childhood summers during the 1940s were spent in the Possum Hollow house. My memories tend toward the Manichean. On one side are idyllic frolics on the property with my dear cousins and our friends, some of them the children of those with whom Betty and Estelle once played hide-and-seek. My Proustian sense memory is the smell of cedar needles. On the other side is my grandfather's slow, excruciating death from cancer, during which the sisters took turns nursing the screaming patient, while we children were warned, as we played on, against making unseemly noise.

# THE BEGINNINGS OF BETTY AND ESTELLE'S EDUCATION

BETTY AND ESTELLE'S schooling followed the pattern of family migration, but approximately in reverse: Jamesburg to New Brunswick to New York City. Although Estelle was the better student, Betty played a key role in Estelle's education.

By the time my mother started, Jean and Harry were already attending the town's one-room schoolhouse—one teacher for eight classes, first to eighth grade. Since mostly Russian and Yiddish were spoken at home ("Russian when they didn't want us to understand"), my mother started school knowing very little English. She also told me she was embarrassed by the hand-me-downs she wore, which were usually too small, and by the fact that she was cross-eyed, because her parents did not want to pay for a corrective operation.

### "Drown of Snow"

**BETTY**: ONE DAY, the boy behind Jean stuck her long hair into his inkwell. The boys said they would "take care of" the culprit after school. On the way out, they threw him in a ditch full of snow. I thought he would drown of snow there. The bus—the wagon—came along, and they pulled him out of the ditch. He'll never forget that.

## Betty's Education, Interrupted

**BETTY**: MY FATHER went into the butter and egg business, [delivering] to New Brunswick. And Jean helped Pop with the butter. Every night. Two or three times a week, my father took me out of school to sit on the truck. Winter, summer. My father had a crank-up truck. He'd bring me lunch. Sometimes, later on, he'd let me deliver a few [orders].

**Estelle**: I can imagine why he took the girls. He was chauvinistic. And I think it was particularly so in the Jewish religion.

**Betty**: Imagine missing your classes, and then having to go back to take the test. I used to pass by the skin of my teeth. And, luckily, I graduated from the eighth grade. By that time, I was able to catch up a little, because Jack was going [to New Brunswick with Sam]. They complained in the school, and they called my parents in. And then they took Jack instead of me. I was an average student. And Jack wasn't as good as me. And Jean was a poor student. She quit in the lower grades.

(At first, my mother seems proud of having been asked to help her father with the deliveries. But, after Estelle's comment, as so often, she changes her tune, deferring to the opinion of her clever younger sister.)

## A BRIEF LIFE OF SANDY (SAM), THE YOUNGEST CHILD

**ESTELLE:** SANDY AND I were in the same class. He was a year younger, but because of our birthdays…up until the third grade. Then, Miss Applegate, our teacher, she was so annoyed—he was the class clown—that she left him back. And when you think back, he was a very bright child. To be left back because he was amusing the class sounds pretty archaic.

(Sandy's life was dogged by misfortune. The cause seems to have been a mixture of softheaded-ness and bad luck. After being jilted by a beauty as a young adult in the Bronx (so the story goes), he moved to Texas. Sandy was a pharmacist by profession. In Texas, he later told me, he was swindled by a partner, and lost his business. He also married a Southern girl, not Jewish. Dying of a heart attack in, I think, his fifties, he was buried in her family cemetery someplace in Louisiana.

Our family was always bitterly divided about whether to accept Sandy's, and other, "mixed" marriages. To my father's credit—at least, in my eyes—he never questioned these marriages. But the Singers were a pack of atheists, both the anarchist and socialist varieties.)

## THE DEATH OF THE FIRSTBORN

AS FOR SAM and Bessie's oldest son, (also) Harry, a promising start in life ended in horror. He married a Canadian first cousin, and after a daughter (Ann) was born with a congenital illness, he turned the gas on, killing her and his wife. What happened after that diverges in family accounts, but they all include Harry's own early death. He may have suffered from what is now called bipolar disorder, the disease that afflicted my sister.

## BETTY & ESTELLE BEGIN TO SPREAD THEIR WINGS

**BETTY**: I WAS about fourteen. I got out of school, and instead of going to high school, he [Sam] took me to take up Beauty Culture in New Brunswick. [Sam suggested a trade because the other option was for his daughter to work in a factory.] So I took up the course, and I did pretty well. And then I went to New Brunswick by bus for a few weekends, and I got a few jobs.

A few years later, to make more money (and, probably, to become more independent), my mother moved to New York. Once she had a job and an apartment, she began to help three of her siblings—Jean, Jack, and Estelle—as they also tried to make their way in Gotham.

## Estelle Follows Her Big Sister

**ESTELLE**: I DIDN'T see any prospects for me in Jamesburg. It was dead. So, in my junior year, I decided to come to New York and stay with you. I registered at the George Washington High School. And the only way I could go to that school—because, geographically, Betty wasn't living in the right area—I was able to give my uncle's address as my home. We had the same name, so it was okay. He was living on 33 Riverside Drive.

**Betty**: When did you take up Beauty Culture?

**Estelle**: I took up Beauty Culture…while I was living in New York with you and going to George Washington High School.

**Betty**: Where did you take it?

**Estelle**: White Academy, on 42$^{nd}$ Street.

**Betty**: So I sent her to Beauty School. At least she had a trade.


## Estelle Completes Her Education (1)

**ESTELLE**: SO I stayed in George Washington High for the whole of my junior year and six months of my senior year. My grades were very good. However, I had no Regents credits. And you know, New York State requires Regents, whereas New Jersey doesn't. To get Regents credits, I would have to review courses I was already finished with, like algebra.

So I went back to Jamesburg. By that time, my family had moved from the Possum Hollow house to an apartment on Hooker Street, where the bowling alley was. By that time, my father was not doing the butter and egg business. It was the Depression. So he opened a[nother] luncheonette.

**Betty**: They didn't need a big house, anymore.

# Hooker Street

SAM OWNED THE Hooker Street building, which, in addition to the bowling alley on the ground floor and a big room rented out for dances and such upstairs, there was the apartment. This was the last dwelling where any of the children lived. It was from here that Estelle left to join Betty in New York, and where she returned to finish high school. After Hooker Street, Bessie and Sam moved to the Bronx for a few years, where Sam owned a food store. After that, the old couple moved back to Jamesburg, exact location unknown.

The Hooker Street building, with a large wooded lot behind it, became "the family property we're always talking about"— possibly the property Grandpa lost during the Depression, possibly because his wealthy brother, whom my family called "Uncle," would not, or could not, lend him money to meet the mortgage payments. Possibly, too, Uncle still owed Sam money for helping him get to the U.S. My father's repeated lampoons of Uncle's posh wife, Aunt Anna, may have been given point by this bitter family story. Like many such stories, however, this one seems incapable of verification. (Until I told it to them, my cousins claimed never to have heard it.) More certain is that, on both sides of my family, most roads lead back to the Depression.

# Estelle Completes Her Education (2)

**ESTELLE**: THE PRINCIPAL reviewed my courses and my marks, and said, "You could graduate with your class." In fact, I was taking three languages, French, Spanish, and English. I have a funny report card from my last year. All As and A+s, but no math or science. Then, I went back to New York.

(Estelle's ardor for education may have descended diagonally to me. However, with a Ph.D. in Renaissance English, and a dozen books under my belt, it would be disingenuous not to note the influence of my father's people. Although, in those days, thwarted education ran on both sides of my family, the Singers overcame more obstacles than did the Kaufmans. The former were widely read leftist intellectuals, whereas the latter tended to stick to the one Good Book—The Bible—and, even more narrowly, the Pentateuch, or *Torah*—i.e., the first five, so-called Mosaic, books of the Old Testament.)

## A POEM ABOUT MY MOTHER

THIS FAIRLY RECENT poem, a knockoff of a sonnet by John Milton (#23, "Me thought I saw my late espoused Saint"), encapsulates my relationship with my mother, both before and after my sister's death.

### I Thought I Saw My Mother, Long Deceased

I thought I saw my mother, long deceased,
standing before the garage door of our home.
While I kicked the ball at her crazily,
careless as to whether I bruised her bones,
face set, arms akimbo, a goalkeeper,
she tried to maintain a stern demeanor.
Later, we became a broken family,
lives shattered when my sister took her own
by throwing herself in front of a train.
My aunt had to go and claim the remains,
for my mother was paralyzed, a wreck.
After that, no more fun: no jokes, no games.
My sad mother never got back on track.

When I'd ask her how she was, "…oh, about the same."

# EPILOGUE:

## WHAT I TOOK

December 22ⁿᵈ, 2013

GRANDMA BETTY WAS no one else's grandmother. I knew and didn't know about her the things one does and does not know about one's grandmother. And I knew through knowing her, as grandchildren often must, that my parents were partial people. My relationship with Grandma Betty was separate from theirs, and I observed them, in their dealings with her, as separate from myself.

The aunt I never met was everywhere in this: Ann, who lived with mental illness and committed suicide in her 20s. Though Ann was never the topic, she was often the reason: why Grandma Betty was no one else's grandmother; why my Dad held an adolescent remove from his mother; surely one of the reasons why Grandma Betty was so entirely…soft. Grandma Betty's ring-indented hands fingering an afghan that she and Ann had made, the very stone of her Florida condominium, across which darted curve-tailed little lizards, the air rolled into her short curly permanent—a child was strong enough to make a mark in these things.

Betty Singer did not have a soft life, and she could not have been soft all her life. She and her sister, like blades of a scissor, made a crossed life of hairdressing, marital submission, and motherhood. Except Betty failed to bring her two children into adulthood. My Great Aunt Estelle was much more definite. Her cooking tasted better and was healthier. She had opinions, and the confidence of having them. There was a subtle step down to her sunken living room that would trip you up and throw you on the floor if you didn't toe the line around her. I loved her, but

Estelle was sharper, more like all the other people in my life. Grandma Betty was unlike any other person in my childhood experience.

Grandma Betty adored and repulsed me, as a flabby and wrinkled old woman with perfumes on a tray outside her bathroom and a love of sweet overcooked food will when you are 7, 8, or 9, visiting over winter break with your parents who are desperately trying to escape, and sometimes sharing a bedroom with her. In a poem I wrote in college, I likened Grandma Betty's skin to the feel of a banana peel.

I was famous in Grandma Betty's condominium, by no virtues of my own. I was petted somewhat like a poodle. I once floated about in the warm, shallow pool, while the ladies crouched weightless in the water in swim-skirt ensembles, keeping their hair dry, and admired my eyebrows to the point of superlative. Grandma Betty gave me a gold horse necklace. She would have done me up if she could: make-up, curlers, and bling. Her walk-in closet was full of pastel culottes and white cotton sweaters with loose open knits. Her underwear drawer housed Mother's Day cards from Ann.

My father took me fishing in the canals near the condominium once, and I caught a turtle, reeling in the ambient guilt that surrounded those trips for him. On the way home, I walked through a red anthill. I was swarmed and tormented, and we ran back to the condo, where my grandmother stripped me and put me in the shower. She was my father's mother, and he had run to her with me for help. She raised her children with fierce care, nursed my Grandpa Harry through decades of anger, high blood pressure, type 2 diabetes, then cancer.

The condo was low lit. A parakeet lived in the cow-themed kitchen for a while. I marveled that my grandmother's oven was full of cereal boxes. And prunes. She tried to interest me in kefir, which I've recently begun stocking and pushing on my family.

The living room was decorated with her paintings, all framed, all copies of the masters, all somewhat mustard in hue. My mother is an abstract artist. Grandma Betty kept a candy dish, naturally, and porcelain figurines on a glass shelf, though these with affection rather than the conviction of a collector. Her palm-sheltered patio was wonderful, white furniture upholstered in just the yellow and green vinyl print you imagine. Looking down, you could watch the occasional adult child jog by, chasing their autonomy while visiting aging parents. And of course, the elderly walkers and bikers. Grandma Betty's bike, a green Raleigh Cruiser, is one of my proudest, and heaviest, possessions.

After she died of lung cancer, perhaps decades after, I first remembered waking up from her living room couch to a horrific sound. I prowled the dark apartment, winding up with my ear to Grandma Betty's bedroom door. She was snoring and gasping. She must have already had cancer. By the time she was diagnosed, she had a couple months at most. Great Aunt Estelle died in the same way. My parents were befuddled about what to take from Grandma Betty's condo. I requested an afghan she'd made. We still use it. I can see it on the couch from where I write. Someone must have napped under it recently.

## 3. GRANDPA SETS THE RECORD STRAIGHT

I MUST HAVE rubbed too much moisturizer on my pate because, in the middle of breakfast, the genie appeared. Before I could protest, he spoke up, the usual smug smile on his Mr. Clean face.

"Hey, Ron. Suppose you could spend an hour with any person, living or dead. Who would you choose?"

"You mean, 'whom.'" I hardly had to think. "My maternal grandfather, Sam Kaufman."

While the genie did his ectoplasmic thing, I put my unfinished breakfast back in the fridge and went to the bathroom to freshen up. The reason I chose Grandpa Sam was simple: I had thought about him so much over the years that my memories had probably turned into myths. They needed a reality check.

Back in the kitchen, the genie was gazing idly at the fridge—idly, because I never offer him anything. (The fact is, I can't stand him.) While we waited for Grandpa's image to materialize, the rotund sprite twiddled his thumbs against his big stomach. Then, glancing at me, he chortled. "Look how nervous you are, Ronald. You're afraid of your own shadow." As he knew, the surest way to get my goat is to use my legal name, which I associate with telephone solicitations and dead relatives.

"Stupid genie," I replied. "What should people be afraid of, if *not* their own shadows?" Apparently, the idea sailed right over his head for, with a shrug, he disappeared. Good riddance (…until I need him again).

By now, my shadow, clear and complete, stood before me.

"Grandpa," I said. "Welcome."

"Thank you." We exchanged awkward little bows.

I had long remembered my maternal grandfather as a gaunt, handsome, tallish old man with a little smile on his bearded face. Resurrected, he looked to be about fifty-five, the age at which he had died. But he was no more than five-and-a-half feet tall. (I'm an even six.)

Whereas I had pictured him in a shiny black gabardine suit, high-buttoned shoes, and a white shirt with a frayed collar (no tie), Grandpa now wore dark woolen pants (it was winter), a gray Cardigan sweater over a brown shirt, and a pair of incongruous red-plush bunny slippers. His feet seemed small, but that may have been the slippers. He still had a neat gray beard, and his hair, too, looked the way I remembered it: long, straight, and, except at the temples, dark. But, whereas I had capped his image with a black yarmulke, he now sported a rakish, forest green Kangol cap.

Remembering my manners, I invited Grandpa into the living room, where we sat down, he in the armchair and I on the couch. I was glad he bore no signs of the excruciating cancer that had killed him. I have no memory of the exact location of the cancer—somewhere in the nether regions—or of his death or funeral. For that matter, I seldom visit the family plot on Staten Island.

"Well, Ranu," he said. "I'm glad to see you again. Has life been good to you?" His voice was still deep and soft. Although I remembered an accent, all that remained of it was the Yiddishized version of my name.

"It has, it has, Grandpa."

Of course, when you haven't seen someone for nearly seven decades, a conventional answer to a sweeping question like that is even more meaningless than when you run into a neighbor on the elevator, and reply to his or her "How you doing?" with "Fine, thanks," or "Can't complain." Still, until my retirement a decade ago, I enjoyed a long and satisfying career as a teacher, and I continue to enjoy my dear family, including a wonderful nine-year old grandson of my own.

"Where have you been, Grandpa? I mean, you've been dead since…1949, wasn't it?"

"1948. 'Where have I been?'" He looked uneasy. "Actually, I'm not permitted to say."

I managed a smile. "Never mind. I didn't invite you here to discuss the afterlife."

"What *was* your purpose, please?" he asked politely.

Not that I remembered Grandpa as a rude man, but neither did I remember him as an especially polite one. Unless a dead relative was extremely rude in life—and there were many such, on both sides of the family—this isn't the sort of thing you remember.

When I explained that my purpose was to do a reality check on my memories, Grandpa laughed. "Okay," he said, "let's do the reality check." He made it sound like a dance. "Do I look the way you remember?"

"Pretty much. Of course, you seem shorter, but that's because I'm much taller than when you were…alive."

"I should hope so. Do you recall my last days, Ranu?"

"I do, I do."

"I bet you mostly remember the screaming. I apologize for that, it must have mortified you, a seven-year old child. I couldn't help it, of course, but it even embarrassed me."

"Do you think I need an apology, Grandpa?"

Instead of replying, he stood up, stepped forward, gave me a warm hug, then sat back down. It surprised me that the dead could touch the living.

"Bladder cancer," he said. "I hear that kind is still difficult to deal with."

It was time to change the subject. "Do you remember how I used to play Store with the Rubenstein girls in the grape arbor behind our house? Did you know about that, Grandpa?"

"Of course. Your grandmother told me. And about how you played Doctor with them, too." When he smiled again, with the trace of a leer, it occurred to me how much sexual mores had changed in seven decades. By now, Grandpa's prurience seemed innocent.

"Estelle and my mom told me stories about you from when they were girls."

He chuckled. "I bet they made me out to be quite a tyrant, a dyed-in-the-wool male chauvinist. Especially Estelle. She was always…advanced."

"Yes, Estelle was critical. She told me how you didn't want her to join that summer arts-and-crafts class at the church. And how she talked you into it, and then made a wood carving of books from the New Testament, and hid it from you."

What the hell? This story couldn't hurt Grandpa now.

He laughed again. "I know about the carving, Ranu. Your grandmother found it when she was cleaning out Estelle's closet." Since Grandma had always been so subservient, I wasn't surprised she had "ratted out" her daughter.

"What did you think?"

He shrugged. "What did I think, or what *do* I think? I thought it was dangerous. But I heard that, last year, Estelle's granddaughter was given a nice *bat mitzvah*—in Portland, Maine, of all places. So I guess the carving didn't do much long-term damage."

"Do you still think it was wrong of her to make it?"

"A difficult question. Generally speaking, Estelle's independence served her well in life. And many people today would call me a bigot."

"But, back then, weren't you afraid she would stop being...Jewish?"

"I was afraid none of my children would remain observant. But, as it happened, all three girls kept the faith pretty well. In fact, my first daughter, Jean, remained strictly observant, despite a lifetime of tribulations. Oh, that reminds me, Ron." Grandpa suddenly looked sheepish. "You left something out, about Jean. I believe she was remarried, quite happily, to a man named Eddie Something."

"Whoa, I forgot that. Eddie Dichter. Nice guy. Thanks, Grandpa. If the book goes to a third edition, I'll have to put him in. And I'll also have to change that sentence about how Jean never put hardship behind her. Huh. But you were saying? About whether all your children remained observant?"

"Oh, yes. Of the boys, Harry and Jack also stayed in the fold. But Sandy…after that lovely girl jilted him in the Bronx, he moved to Texas, and wound up marrying a *shik*…a *gen*…a Christian…he's buried in a Baptist cemetery in Louisiana." Grandpa sighed and looked philosophical. "Oh, well."

"Have you seen him lately?"

"I'm not allowed to say. But, if you're curious, ask that genie of yours to go get him."

"Nah," I joked, "my account is overdrawn." My curiosity about Sandy had never been keen.

Grandpa looked sheepish again. "Then maybe I should leave," he said. "I don't want to run up the bill."

"No, no, Grandpa. I sent for you." I was relieved he had not mentioned my own recusancy.

"Thanks." He winked. "But why not ask me about things that come closer to the gritty-nitty?"

I had just learned something new about Grandpa, whom I had never thought of as a playful man. Before getting to the "gritty-nitty," I offered him a choice of non-alcoholic beverages (since I remembered that, in life, the only alcohol he had allowed to pass his lips was bad wine, on holidays). When he refused, the next question rolled off my tongue so readily that it surprised even me.

"When Grandma needed new shoes, did you really leave her home, shoeless, and take her old pair back to the city to buy the same ones?"

Grandpa scowled. "Who told you that nonsense, Ranu? Look, someone had to stay home to care for the chickens and the younger children. Besides, Grandma had other shoes—and slippers. Your grandmother never went barefoot. What do you think we were, peasants?"

"Understood," I muttered. "I apologize."

"Speak up, Ranu. And hurry. We're still on the meter."

"What's the rush, Grandpa? Do you have eggs to deliver?"

He smiled sweetly. "Butter, too. No, Ron, I don't do that, anymore. I'm 'retired,' remember?" His sudden switch to the modern form of my name surprised me. Grandpa was full of surprises.

"Okay. Then, is it true you made my mother miss school to help you with the deliveries to New Brunswick?"

"Not just New Brunswick. We delivered to Englishtown, Hightstown, Spotswood, Possum Hollow, several other places. It was a business, not a game." He looked angry again. "But isn't your real question why I took your mother, instead of one of the boys?" I shrugged. "Well, that's how things were in those days. Boys went to school longer, unless the girls showed particular promise. Your mother was an average student at best. Besides, later, I sometimes took Jack. And I didn't pull Estelle out of school, did I? And when your mom wanted to spread her wings and move to New York on her own, did I stop her?"

"I bet you tried."

Grandpa's expression grew stormy. "Uh, oh," he said. "Are we going to start fighting now?" He made a visible effort to control himself. "Things change, Ron. Hindsight is a form of ignorance. As an educated man, you should know that. When *you* die, do you want *your* grandson to judge *you?*"

"You're right, Grandpa. Let's change the subject. That day you stopped the guy in the car who was trying to kidnap me...do you remember that?"

"How could I forget it?"

"You may have saved my life. If I never properly thanked you, Grandpa, I thank you now."

He shrugged. "Don't mention it. People say the world has grown more dangerous, but it was plenty dangerous, then." He looked into my eyes. "And you know what else, Ron? I think you wanted to go off with that kidnapper."

"I did. According to the story, as I heard it, he lured me by promising to buy me ice cream in town."

"You were four years old, and that could have been the end of you. I don't think they ever caught the bastard, either. Maybe, you could ask that genie of yours to summon him from Hell…but I doubt you'd want to see him again."

"Calm down, Grandpa. Can I make you a sandwich, or something? A cup of tea?"

He sighed. "Thanks, Ron. Even as a child, you were generous. But eating and drinking are not permitted." He drew his old-fashioned timepiece from a pocket of his sweater. "Besides, your wife will be home soon." How did he know that? "And since I'm not authorized to speak with her, I really should be on my way. By the way, when are you going to write something about the Singers, your father's family?"

"Who knows? It might have to be fiction; I've been estranged from that side of the family for years."

"I see. I knew a lot of them, you know. Not just your dad. His brother, Aaron, his nephew, Wally—good people."

"Mm-hmm. One more question, please. I've been thinking about this ever since you got here."

"Ha!" Grandpa looked sly. "I could see there was something you were having trouble spitting out. This one must be a doozy."

"After six children, did you and Grandma stop…sleeping together?"

"What? Of course not. We only had one bed." He laughed heartily at his own joke. "No, my boy, we didn't stop. We were a normal couple, not even old yet."

"But what about the prohibitions against…"

With a completely straight face, he interrupted. "Ronald, your grandmother and I adhered strictly to the esteemed liberal teachings in the rabbinical tradition."

Using that as his exit line, before I could stop laughing, or say goodbye, Grandpa vanished. I went back to the kitchen, warmed up my half-eaten breakfast, and made myself a cup of tea—which was odd, since I never drink the stuff.

* * *

AROUND FOUR A.M., when I was in my deepest sleep, the genie turned up again.

"Well? How'd it go?"

This genie is like hospitals and all those other officious entities that badger you to "rate your experience."

"Shh, you'll wake my wife." She was curled up next to me, facing the wall in her own deep sleep.

He lowered his voice to a whisper. "What did you think of him?"

"He was fine. Look, send me the bill. Let me sleep in peace now."

"I hope you didn't believe everything he said."

That woke me up, all right. "What? Would Grandpa's ghost lie?"

"Sure. As one of the keepers of his reputation, you're his shadow. He'd lie because he was afraid of you."

I could feel the genie's amorphous aura shaking with mirth.

**The End**

# POSTSCRIPT

## Broccoli Rabe, Broccoli Rasta

...sang the radio in Accra,
as we bumped along from where to where.
"What's that?" I asked the driver.
"It sounds like reggae, but..."
"*Ivoirien* reggae."
"Ohhh, that's why...ah-ha."

On the day I broke my foot,
lost an eye, and didn't say
"Good morning" to my wife,
Leo, three, grinned at me.
"Grandpa," he said.
"What is it, my dear?"
"Broccoli Rabe, Broccoli Rasta."

### The End

# ACKNOWLEDGMENTS

(Note that some of the original texts have been modified to fit the needs of *Gravy.*)

(in order of appearance):

"There are few things I hate…" —from *A Voice for My Grandmother* (Ten Penny Players/BardPress Chapbooks, (2006; second printing, 2008), and currently available from the publisher as a free PDF (www.tenpennyplayers.org.) *Betty and Estelle* is available online at Piker Press. *Ranu M'zooka* is hitherto unpublished.

"2012," from "Two Pairs of Pants," *Earl of Plaid,* 2015.

"Secrets of the Boardwalk," *Jonah*, Jan. 15, 2017: jonahmagazine.com/2017/01/15/secrets-of-the-boardwalk/

"Pocketbook Money Keys," *Word Ways: The Journal of Recreational Linguistics*, June 2018.

"Other People's Clothes," *New Pop Lit,* 2017.

*Rimshot* (libretto, with Russell Currie, composer), performed at Pace University Downtown Theater Summer Festival, NY, 1990.

"The Actuarialist," *diagram* (online), 4.6, January 2005 & 2005 print anthology.

"Dante's Way," *Boned, A Collection of Skeletal Writings*, January 21, 2020.

"Reader, I Read to Him," online serial in Piker Press, beginning June 4, 2018: http://www.pikerpress.com/article.php?aID=6121

 "The Tigers of Yerevan," from "The Hillendale Hobby Club, Parts 1-3," *Home Planet News*, Issue #6, Fall 2018: http://www.homeplanetnews.org/AOnLine.html.

"Tigers" was first published in *Evergreen* Review, 2014.

"The Real Enemy Within," *Home Planet News*, Issue #5, 2018.

"Living in the Moment," *big bridge*, summer 2012.

"The Old Boy Lunch Club," *Strong Verse, November 15, 2013:* http://www.strongverse.org/.

"The Parents We Deserve," *Ellipsis*, 2006 (print), & *nth position*, 2009, online (Part One only); *The Second Kingdom, three novellas, Cantarabooks*, 2009; jukepopserials.com, 2013; Piker Press, 2016; Kindle Books, 2017.

"Brown, the Concept," *Avatar Review*, 2016.

Chapter One of "I, Muffin," was published in *Fiction Week Literary Review*, Apr. 2015. The whole story has ten chapters and an Epilogue.

"Kith and Kindred," *The Creative Truth*, 2017.

"My Father-in-Law, Eighty-Eight," *Puckerbrush Review*, Summer/Fall 2001.

"I Thought I Saw My Mother, Long Deceased," one of a set of four 'Miltonic" poems, *Ascent Aspirations*, November 2015.

"Broccoli Rabe, Broccoli Rasta," *Grey Sparrow*, 2012; *River Poets Journal (postcard poems)*, 2014; *Poetry Atlas*, 2015.

In a modified form, "IBS Rides the Internet" is included in *The Real Presence* (Adelaide Books, 2021), a historical novel about Nigeria.

# About the Author

Ron Singer, b.1941, has been both a lifelong resident of New York City, and one who has traveled to, lived in, and written about the wider world. For forty-four years, Singer was a teacher and writer. Singer's life and writing have both featured political activism. For instance, while he was in South Africa working on a book, he was invited to read poetry at a memorial for activist/poet Dennis Brutus. The book is *Uhuru Revisited: Interviews with Pro-Democracy Leaders* (Africa World Press, Red Sea Press, 2015). It can be found in libraries around the world.

# About the Press

Unsolicited Press is a small press in Portland, Oregon. The team produces poetry, fiction, and creative nonfiction written by emerging and award-winning authors.

Learn more at www.unsolicitedpress.com.